HACKED

Tracy Alexander lives in Bristol with three teenagers, no pets, one husband, one jukebox, three bicycles and one unicycle she can't ride.

HACKED

TRACY ALEXANDER

Piccadilly

First published in Great Britain in 2014
by Piccadilly Press
Northburgh House, 10 Northburgh Street,
London, EC1V 0AT
www.piccadillypress.co.uk

A catalogue record for this book is available
from the British Library

ISBN: 978 1 84812 414 1

3 5 7 9 10 8 6 4

Printed in the UK by Clays Ltd, St Ives Plc

Piccadilly Press is part of the Bonnier Publishing Group
www.bonnierpublishing.com

Thanks to James the hacker, Seal the brain,
Mike the judge, Rob the logician, Felix the sceptic,
Honor the meticulous, Oscar the plotter,
steady Jess and the three ugly sisters.

PART 1

1

You should have seen the look on Soraya's face.

'You bought me credit?'

'Not exactly,' I said.

'Come on, Dan. I've got like fifty quid on my phone out of nowhere.'

I wasn't that keen to spell it out.

'I ... took advantage of a ... loophole.'

'You mean ...'

I nodded — a small nod, understated. No need to crow.

'No way!' She kissed me on the cheek, right by the school gates.

Ty whistled. Juvenile.

'I never thought going out with a computer nerd would come with *benefits*,' she said. Huge smile.

'All in a day's work.' I shrugged as I said it, hating myself for talking in clichés.

'Thanks so much, Dan. Got to go. I'll message you *all* night.'

She wouldn't. Soraya was always at Mia's or Claire's or a hundred other friends' houses. I should have chosen a less social girlfriend, but to be honest, *I* didn't really choose. She sort of chose me. And even though it was all on her terms, I was happy to go along with it. Big brown eyes, caramel skin, no spots, nice lips – what's not to like?

'Coming?' said Ty.

'Aren't we waiting for Joe?' I said.

'He's climbing.'

We set off home. A lot of our year go to the park but hanging around by the baby swings doesn't do it for me. Or Ty – he's too busy being 'destined for great things'. And Joe – he's just busy. Current fad – bouldering at the climbing centre wearing weird shoes with a separate toe compartment.

'I got my work experience sorted,' said Ty.

'What are you doing, assisting with a lobotomy?'

He wants to be a neurosurgeon, all because he saw an operation on the telly where they cut into someone's brain while they were awake. Gross.

'I'm shadowing Jenna Wade's aunty,' he said. 'She does hip replacements.'

'Start at the bottom,' I said, but he didn't get the joke.

He was made up. Me, I was planning on a week off. That's the thing with hacking. An official email stating I had a placement with a vet, a lawyer, the police (ha!), Tesco's – all within my grasp.

'Saw Soraya all over you,' he said.

'It's nature, Ty. They're attracted to the fittest specimens.'

Pretty funny! I'm anything but. Rake thin – I like that

expression, a pole with lots of teeth at the top (or maybe the same number as everyone else). White – I don't mean race, I mean not enough daylight. Eyes of a loon – too much screen time. That's not actually true. It's one of the stupid things parents say, and even more weird, seem to believe. Computers do not make your eyes bloodshot. No sleep makes your eyes bloodshot, and getting shampoo in them.

Anyway, enough about me. That day, the day I presented Soraya with her stolen credit, was the start of it. I didn't know, but then you never do. It's the butterfly effect thing, the one tiny flutter that causes a tsunami the other side of the world.

2

Strictly speaking the start was years and years before
– that's what Mum would say if she was listening. Not
that she would be, because we don't really talk. I like her
and all that, but there's a reason why sixteen-year-olds
aren't friends with middle-aged women (hold any cougar
comments) and it's that they have nothing in common.

Anyway, I was trouble. Not burn-the-school-down
sort of trouble. More like eczema, an irritating itch
– maybe infected. By the juniors, I'd been paraded
in front of the doctor, a psychiatrist or two *and* a
cranial osteopath. (I liked that. She held my head.) I
could have told them why I fiddled, fidgeted, didn't pay
attention, and talked over everyone, but they don't
ask *you* – far too obvious. They try to tease it out by
clever tests like seeing if you trash a tower of bricks
they 'accidentally' leave in the room. Seriously, I don't
recommend anyone take a kid to a 'professional'. Gran
had the diagnosis all along.

'He's too bright for his own good.'

That wasn't the general conclusion. ADHD was. And
I got a prescription for white pills to help me 'focus'. I

was like nine or something. My offences were mostly to do with taking things apart, like the battery-operated pencil sharpener, or arguing with Mr Fellows, usually about dinosaurs and meteorites. Poor Mr Fellows – I went dressed as a policeman on World Book Day (no idea why), complete with handcuffs, and locked him to the door handle. There was a quick release button but he sent me to the Head before I could tell him. Got excluded for that.

The pills were fine, nice in fact, but the real antidote to all my anti-social behaviour came in the form of a computer.

Ta-da! Happy eleventh birthday, Dan.

A battery-operated pencil sharpener reduced to its components was no match for the *internet*. Websites can be made to do something else, or made better, or taken down. Endless possibilities. I was a reformed character – a 'model' student', apparently. In reality I was either thinking about stuff I shouldn't do, or doing it.

The first what you'd call 'proper' hack was for my little sister, El, short for Elena. She was already on the free bit of Club Penguin (not cool, but true) meeting friends with terrible names like Penny5925 and Aceman09 on the Iceberg and tipping it over, but she wanted to be a member. The parents wouldn't pay the subscription so I had a tinker and next thing she had her Member Stamp. That meant she could buy things with 'coins'. So I got her some. A shedload. I don't like to think of that as a crime. It's a crime to advertise to little girls knowing they don't have their own money.

In my next review at the doctors I realised I should have been a bit less 'model', because they took me off the pills and declared me cured. A few twitches and a quick rummage through the equipment in the surgery would have swung it, but for once I hadn't anticipated what might happen. You can buy the stuff online anyway. Not that I ever bothered. Better things to do. Following threads, joining forums, finding holes, fixing them, coding some scripts to improve the odds of winning free competitions, as well as the odd dodgy thing like hacking free cinema tickets, and, of course, endless gaming. There was a blip when I accidentally drew attention to myself by hacking the control unit on Dad's BMW. We live on a narrow-ish street that people use as a cut-through and passing cars are always hitting the wing mirrors, so I helpfully made them fold in automatically whenever it was parked. Quite chuffed with that, I was. Until the parents confronted me. I said someone else showed me how to do it. Thankfully they were so pleased not to have to deal with a 'medicated' child any more they chose to believe me.

I'd have carried on quite happily as a hobby hacker, messing with whatever caught my eye along with all the other anonymous grey hats who like code, if it hadn't been for Soraya.

3

Soraya arrived at the start of Year Ten – covered in glitter and sparkle – but I didn't speak to her until we were partnered up in biology to dissect a sheep's eye, approximately four weeks before the generous act that started my downfall and around eighteen months after I first saw her.

'Will you do it, Dan?' she said – stereotypically squeamish girl.

'Sure.' Manly Dan!

'Only my nails aren't dry.'

We identified the main parts and then I had to cut away the fat and muscle. A wave of weird came over me. I breathed a lot.

'You OK?' she said.

'Fine.'

'Cut it then.' She was waving her hands, encouraging the second coat of iridescent purple to dry.

The sheep's cornea was looking up at me. I put the scalpel against the sclera and pushed. A glug of clear liquid came out and spilled over my gloved finger.

I heard, 'That's the aqueous humour.'

Embarrassing isn't the word. I came round, aware I had chin dribble, to find her diamond-pierced nose right over my face. She burst out laughing, a good noise — like a sleigh bell.

'Did I . . . faint?'

'Only for a second,' she said. 'Don't worry, I'll do the rest.' She blew her nails. 'They're dry now.'

'Everything all right there?' said Mrs Dean, looking over but not bothering to heave her huge body out of the chair.

'We're good,' said Soraya.

She proceeded to cut the eye in half, remove the cornea, cut that in two — which made a hideous crunching sound and nearly sent me weird again — and then pull the iris out with her painted fingernails. Soraya wasn't *squeamish*, she was vain. She also wasn't wearing her latex gloves, but it was past the point where it mattered.

'There's the pupil,' she said, dangling the iris in front of me.

She fished a clear lump out of the back of the eye and held it in her palm.

'Lens,' she said, grinning.

How I was feeling wasn't lost on her. She held up the lens for me to look through. There was a bit of glob hanging off it. I shut my eyes.

'You're a wuss,' she said.

'Agreed.'

You'd think being brave and macho would be the way to get a girl, but Soraya ... she fell for my weak stomach. It happened without any of the escalating steps I'd imagined – chatting, flirting, holding hands, *finally* a snog. That same day we went to the canteen together and I watched her eat tuna pasta. (My appetite had taken a knock.) Ty and Joe came and sat with us, and then her BFF Mia. I walked her to the bus stop after school and she kissed me on the cheek. A week and a frenzy of texts later, I had a proper girlfriend. (And yes, she did write 'cba', 'lol', 'sup'.) (And no, I did not tease her, despite the many happy hours Joe, Ty and I had spent dissing textspeak.) (Conclusion: we're full of crap.)

Unbelievably, Soraya had to share a computer with her sister, so Skyping and messaging on Facebook were tricky. And her phone was constantly out of credit. That's why I sorted it. I could have pretended that I topped her up with my own money, but I had no idea what was going to happen next. Girls, they're a different species.

4

'Can you put some credit on Mia's phone?' she said, between mouthfuls of popcorn. I was studying the ad for a nice-looking convertible that was either speeding down the wiggly mountain road on rails or entirely Photoshopped. It was our second cinema visit and, like last time, I was hoping not to see too much of the film.

'No.'

'What do you mean "no"?'

Arguing with Soraya was like arguing with Dad. No logic. No reasoning. No gradual raising of voices. Nought to sixty via nowhere.

'Soraya, it's illegal. I magicked fifty quid onto your phone. I don't want everyone knowing that.'

'It's not like you took five tenners out of someone's pocket.'

'It's *exactly* like that.'

'No it's not. It's like they dropped the money on the floor and you picked it up. You're just being mean, Dan. How am I going to tell her that you can't be bothered to shove in the code or whatever it is?'

Great! Throw it back in my face.

'Who else have you told?'

'Only Jasmine.'

Note the 'only'.

Soraya did the whole sob story thing – Mia had a decrepit wind-up phone, an evil mum and no hair straighteners. Whatever! I gave in, not because I'm soft, but because I didn't want a row. I wanted to put my arm round her and taste the popcorn she'd just eaten.

I got what I wanted, and so did Mia. But I made it clear it was a one-off. She was over-the-top grateful.

One-off. Ha!

Girls like to talk. Girls change their BFF every week. Girls are constantly taking selfies and posting them. Girls chew through data. A phone to a girl is not for talking or even texting, it's a body part. When word got round Soraya's millions of friends that I could get free credit, Old Dan – nice eyelashes (long, dark), good at maths, witty (just telling it how it is), not bothered about almost everything – morphed into New Dan – exactly the same. Except everyone wanted to know New Dan, invite him to the party, 'hang out' with him.

This is tricky to explain. I know right from wrong, but I seem to have my own definition of 'wrong'. Kicking someone's head in is wrong. Fleecing a few hundred quid off a mobile phone operator – not so bad. Fleecing a few hundred quid, or in fact much more, and not making any money yourself – stupid. So I introduced a fee. Twenty per cent – strictly cash.

An entirely random figure based on not wanting to think of myself as greedy. Translated for customers that found percentages a challenge, that meant I'd obtain ten pounds of credit on any phone number I was given for the paltry payment of two quid. Everybody wins. The King of Pay As You Go was born.

Even though I was careful about where I hacked from – spoofing IP addresses – it was no surprise (and a bit of a relief) when the top-up site identified the loophole and closed it down after seven weeks. It would make me sound good if I said the guilt was getting to me but it was more that it took up too much time, and I didn't like being hassled to get credit for people's Twitter followers, cats, dead aunts and daemons. You meet crazies, you really do.

So, all in all, the upside was that I made enough money to buy an Alienware laptop. The downside was that there were lots of downsides.

One, Soraya got bored with me always being on my phone or laptop and replaced me with a different model – boy-band haircut, nice teeth, alcohol problem, judging by his photos. I hacked his email, cancelled his memberships of everything from Netflix to the Monterey Aquarium and popped my favourite pics of his (the most embarrassing) up on Facebook. Quite satisfying.

Two, Ty disapproved big time. He stopped waiting for me after school – said he didn't want to be friends with the 'criminal underclass'. It didn't matter to start with, because I had Soraya and all the groupies who wanted favours, and I thought he'd cave, but when it was all over I had to crawl my way back into his good books. (Joe, on the other hand, was a good customer but told me not to tell Ty.)

Three, the world — or at least the bit of it that lived in Bristol and was between twelve and twenty-something — got to know me, and knew I was a law-breaker. That's not great — people still cross the road to avoid me.

Four, the virtual world got to know me too, although not as Dan. The odd comment and, I may as well admit it, the occasional late-night boast, caught the attention of a few other like-minded individuals with strange user names — DarkStar, Immortal Jackal, Expendable, Angel, Viper, Anaconda, Hackingturtle, Plumber, Stoker, Joker, Airdreamer. I was King Penguin, thanks to El. But I quickly shortened it to KP — like the peanuts. It was good to swap a few new exploits, some lines of code, ridicule other people's security and spot the script kiddies trying, but failing, to keep up. There was a community feel to it all, like being in a football team but without the football. One weirdo, too young to be mixing with the likes of us, even tried to pre-order from me!

for my birthday which is in May please can I have some birthday credit I will be 11 I like your name

Technically I'd done the equivalent of robbing a bank, but there are black hats out there doing much worse —

destroying stuff for the hell of it. I wasn't worried. But I should have been. Because the one called Angel liked the look of me. If I could time travel, I'd nip back and warn myself – *stay away from Angel.*

5

Before I go any further, I should explain that I'm not a scary kid with a dysfunctional family living in a squat, everyone on benefits and crack. I've got a mum and dad that I got all my genes from (or so they say), and a sister, one car and a house with three bedrooms. No police records, alcoholics, gambling problems between us. There was nothing that the press could find, when it got to that point, to explain away what I did. Because there was no 'reason'. It was like a row of dominoes, all standing in line until one was pushed over by the wind, and that made the rest tumble. Like that, except slower.

The next domino to fall was Ty.

I found out about the accident through a retweeted tweet and then via every other sort of social media. According to his brothers, Ty was cycling home, stopped at a red light and the bloke behind (need I add, in a white van) jumped the lights, knocking him off and not even stopping to see if he was alive. Unreal. He was in hospital with 'head injuries' – how severe depended on who, of the ten million people from school that texted, messaged and tweeted, you believed. I was furious, actually wanted to punch something, which is not like me. I left my bedroom and searched out a parent, that's how mad I was.

Dad was eating a packet of Bourbons, watching a box set of some crime drama. We could torrent it for free but he's old-fashioned like that. It was Wednesday so Mum had gone to choir.

'Hi.'

'Dan, nice to see you out of your den. What's wrong? Internet down?'

What is it about parents? They say teenagers can't communicate but when you try, they wind you up.

'I do leave my room, Dad. But there's this thing called homework.' I used a sarcastic tone, always goes down well.

'Stea-dy.'

I hate it when he says that, like he's a horse whisperer and I'm about to bolt.

'Can't I have a joke?' he said, eating another biscuit to maintain his XL waist measurement.

'A joke would be fine, Dad. But by definition they have to be funny.'

I changed my mind about telling him and went into the kitchen instead, where El was playing Club Penguin on Mum's computer.

'Can you buy me a new igloo with a pink bed?' she said.

'Depends.'

'On what?' she said.

'On whether you want to make *me* a hot chocolate?'

'Deal,' she said. I went back to my room and topped up her Icelandic bank account.

But she didn't honour her side, because Dad did.

'Ty's dad just rang,' he said, putting down the mug. 'He's been in an accident.'

I didn't say anything, suddenly afraid that he might be dead and I might blub. Not something I'd done since Grandad died.

The last time I saw Grandad he told Gran he wanted 'An oak coffin with brass handles'. And when she went to get a cup of tea he said, 'Pop my tobacco in, Dan, just in case I fancy a smoke.' I laughed, which was what he wanted me to do. And when they buried him I made sure there was some Old Holborn in his jacket pocket.

Dad pushed aside some dirty clothes, loads of chocolate wrappers and a magazine, so he could sit down on the edge of my bed, feet between a pile of plates covered with toast crumbs and a Star Wars poster that fell down when I was about ten. Credit where it's due, he managed not to rant about the mess.

'Ty hasn't come round yet,' he said. 'But that's common, they say. Your brain shuts down to get on with mending itself.'

In biology, Mrs Dean said the brain is like soft tofu. To get that image out of my head, I decided to risk speaking.

'I can't believe it. He was on his way home from

helping at Scouts, you know ... it's part of his Duke of Edinburgh.'

'They should put cameras in their vans,' said Dad, 'to record the bloody awful driving. That would sort them out.'

We carried on talking about how unfair it was, until the million-dollar question found its way out of my mouth.

'Do you think he's going to be all right?'

'I don't know,' said Dad.

I'd have been better asking El – she's the one who watches *Casualty* and checks everyone's symptoms in the *Family Medical Encyclopedia*.

'I'll call round theirs tomorrow, after work,' he said, ruffling my hair, which is about as affectionate as it gets. 'Positive thinking, eh?'

I nodded. Dad disappeared, fatherly duty done.

It's clear to me what goes on in his head, even though he has no clue what goes on in my mine. He feels guilty because he lets me spend so much time in my 'den' but he can't be bothered to do anything about it. He *thinks* we should be up on the Downs kicking a ball, or watching classic films from the 80s or fishing on a river bank like Mole and Ratty, but we'd both rather be on our own than together. Every so often he has a go about me lazing about in the pit that's my room, as well as my general lack of application. I look as though I'm listening, and we carry on like nothing's been said. Works for us.

I went online, keen to think about anything but Ty. And there was Angel, somewhere in the cloud.

We were already friends by then. It's strange the way you can work out who you get on with without eye contact, body language, piercings or a voice to help. It's better in a way – no prejudice about being fat, old, ugly, Vietnamese, blue-tinged, speaking like Sean Connery or Stephen Hawking, or mute. I had no idea whether Angel was fifty, or sixteen like me, whether he had a faith, or if he played polo for England, but I liked him. He was smart, cocky, and the only person, apart from Soraya and Mia, that I didn't charge for credit when I was running the phone scam. It wasn't generosity – I didn't want a money trail over the internet. And I suppose I was showing off. He was stoked:

sweet – good job KP

I actually sent him the lines of code for him to help himself. Kind of me, and it made a sort of bond. After all, I was on the wrong side of the law, and I trusted him not to tell.

Angel was gutted when I told him about Ty's accident:
bad job

I told him I was already dreading going to school and hearing all the girls going over the top, weeping and wailing – **omg! omg!**

dont go – he said.

6

I got dressed in uniform and went downstairs at the normal time, Mum took El to breakfast club on her way to work, Dad took himself, and I went back to my room. Peasy.

I met Angel online and we spent ages baiting other ships in *EVE* with small cruisers, hacked so they could deal out insane damage – it was hilarious. We moved onto *Starcraft II*, and with a little mod of the code to give us unlimited resources, built hundreds of siege tanks and annihilated everyone. That was a good day. In between we chatted about random stuff ... and less random:

hack the council security cameras – get the reg of the van

You'd have thought I could have come up with that idea myself.

might just do that – I typed.

Knowing I could have a crack at finding the idiot who hit and ran made me feel entirely different. Who doesn't like the idea of revenge?

I went out well before the time El comes back from school, and got back home as usual, about four o'clock.

'How was your day, Dan?' asked Mum. She smiled. As mums go, she's up there – cooks nice food, sorts out my clothes and leaves them in a pile outside my room, leaves the inside of my room well alone, leaves me alone.

'Fine,' I said.

'I made banana muffins at school,' said El, pointing at the plate.

'They look great.' I took one and made this-is-delicious noises to please her.

'I'm working tonight,' said Mum. 'So are you all right to take El in the morning?'

She's ten, but hasn't worked out roads *at all*.

'Sure,' I said.

'Thanks, Dan.' Mum put her hand on my shoulder. 'Have you heard anything more about Ty?'

I shook my head. No point sharing the crap everyone was posting.

'Dad's going to pop round there later.'

I nodded, drank a glass of blackcurrant and went up to my room.

I prepared for the task by tidying a rectangle of my desk, loading a random episode of *QI* on my fixed computer, and positioning the laptop bang in the middle. Good to go!

I wasn't expecting the local council's traffic department to be much of an obstacle. And I was right. Two episodes, one loo stop and a Diet Coke later, I'd got inside the system, *and* found the right camera – by the traffic lights on Westbury Road. But there was a problem I hadn't predicted. I could see the live feed, but not the history. For a while I watched the traffic – it's more interesting than you'd imagine. Drivers on the phone, swerving, arguing, last-minute braking, eating – if what I saw was typical, there should be more accidents.

A bad mood was descending. I don't like not being able to figure things out. And this was important. There was a man sitting at home somewhere enjoying a can of beer, while Ty was in a hospital bed attached to pipes and tubes. The CCTV had to be archived somewhere ... I trawled through, getting nowhere, confounded by two common problems – people aren't logical, and systems get added to. (Ironically the same problems that baffle you, sometimes let you in.)

Here's an example of source code:

```
import socket sock = socket.socket(socket.
AF_INET, socket.SOCK_STREAM) sock.
connect(("irc.freenode.com", 6697))
nickname = "NICK Eschaton\r\n"
encoded_nick = bytes(nickname, 'utf-8')
sock.send(encoded_nick)
request username = "USER Neo {0}
Neo :m4tr1c3s\r\n".format(server)
encoded_user = bytes(username, 'utf-8')
sock.send(encoded_user)
```

They're a set of orders, like a flow chart, that you can

manipulate, or add your own commands to. It's like telling a story . . . no, more like telling lots of stories at once. I showed Joe back in the Club Penguin days but he couldn't grasp what I was on about. It's funny because he's clever enough, but there are different types of clever. There's the man in the veg shop who can add the prices of the carrots and sweet potatoes Mum buys in his head, and there's Derren Brown who totally gets how people think, and Joe who can scale a wall like a gecko, and then there's geeks like me – code just makes sense.

Except the archive of the council CCTV didn't make sense. I got the feeling no one ever needed access to footage from the past and it was dumped somewhere offline, never to be seen again. Maybe they erased it . . .

Dad came home at about seven-thirty and called me down. El came too, presumably for medical research purposes. Dad had chatted to Ty's mum and then stayed to look after Ty's twin brothers while his mum and dad swapped roles. They were taking it in turns to keep a bedside vigil because Ty hadn't woken up. He was conscious immediately after the collision but then his brain had shut down because of a bleed.

'Haematoma,' said El.

'It's a matter of time,' said Dad.

Not what I wanted to hear.

'How long?'

'Piece of string, I'm afraid,' said Dad.

'Better shut down than dead,' said El, cheerily. Please

let her not qualify as a doctor.

'I said you'd visit,' said Dad.

Instant panic. I wanted him to get better *obviously*, but the idea of talking to an unconscious Ty freaked me out. You must have seen it on telly – playing their favourite songs, holding hands, chatting as though there was someone listening. No way could I do that.

'OK,' I heard myself say.

'Tomorrow all right with you ... after tea?'

I nodded, hoping I'd get a contagious disease overnight ...

Back in my room, I decided to check through the council's system once more and, like in all good stories, just when I was about to give up and make some toast, I stumbled upon the right server and found the video records. All I had to do was specify the exact co-ordinates, date and time of the accident. Piece of cake. I braced myself, knowing I was about to watch my friend be flattened by a lunatic driver ... but the camera was pointing the wrong way. I could see Westbury Road, the lights and the bus stop, but all the action was past the place where Ty was knocked off.

Total waste of time. The adrenalin that had built up – seeing myself presenting the identity of the criminal to the police and being thanked by Ty's family (ignoring the illegality of hacking for now) – disappeared, and left me feeling pretty flat. To forget about it all I went in search of my elite friends in the virtual playground and offloaded. It was great being able to admit to hacking something without anyone judging:

got the camera but not the crash

was it a long job? – Angel asked.

took 2 episodes *QI* – Pretty cool response, though I say so myself.

maybe try the spy satellite network

I thought Angel was joking. Reconnaissance satellites are controlled by governments. We're talking the Pentagon!

Funny how an idea takes hold ...

7

As I walked El to school she filled me in on Ty's condition, based on Googling 'head injury'.

'Memory problems, headaches, and sometimes vision is affected – that's seeing. If he gets epilepsy they operate. I watched one on YouTube.'

'Bye, El. Have a good day.'

It occurred to me that putting some brotherly controls on her login might be an idea.

'Do you have a note, Dan?' asked Mr Richards as I strolled in, a couple of minutes late. I'd totally forgotten that I'd bunked school so didn't have an excuse ready.

'No. Forgot, sorry.'

'But you're better today?'

'Yes. Twenty-four-hour thing,' I said, head deep in my locker.

'Don't worry this time,' he said.

He obviously thought I'd stayed off because of Ty, who was the subject of *all* the talk. I didn't join in. Half the people that were going on didn't even like him. In popularity terms Ty was about as in demand as I was since Pay As You Go folded.

'You all right?' said Soraya. It was the first time she'd spoken to me since the 'you're dumped' text (**this isnt working for me . . . im breaking up with u sorry**).

'I suppose so,' I said. I wanted to ask her if she was still seeing the boy-band clone but . . .

'I'm sure he'll get better.' She flashed me a celebrity smile complete with glossy lips, before catching up with the other girls. I walked from English to chemistry on my own. Without Ty, who I have most of my classes with, there wasn't anyone obvious to talk to. The nice kids – the ones that wouldn't dream of buying stolen credit – tended to keep away from me. The cool ones, ditto, but for different reasons.

I spent the lesson immersed in a textbook, where my cleverly concealed laptop taught me everything there is to know about satellites, most of it wrong. Here's a selection:

- they're cameras in the sky
- there are loads of different types – weather, search and rescue, navigation, reconnaissance (spying), communications (telly, phone, radio) and military (more spying)
- the Russian *Sputnik* was first, scared the 'pants' off the Americans
- some of them sweep round the earth once a day (some don't)
- they can identify the make and model of a car from

    hundreds of miles high
- they're controlled from base stations on the ground
- there are thousands, mostly used for broadcasting
- exact numbers and nature of military satellites is a secret
- exact numbers of non-military is anything from 2,000 to 16,000, but if you include space junk it's more
- a satellite is actually an object that moves round a larger object e.g. the moon

Conclusions:
- there's loads of rubbish on the internet
- I like lists.

By the time I got home I knew enough to get started. It was crazy to even consider it, but in your room, on your own, playing with IP connections, it doesn't feel like you're doing anything wrong. In fact, you could call hacking a public service. Admittedly, black hats are either out to cause chaos or filch thousands, but there are white hats working hard to make things better simply because they can. And if it weren't for people like me (in the middle – more of a grey hat) governments and big business (like mobile phone operators) wouldn't know how fragile their systems are. And the man in the street wouldn't know that the Americans and the British are listening in to his private conversations.

Spooooky!

Anyway, what were the chances of me cracking it?

8

'Dinner's on the table,' shouted Mum. Her third attempt to get us downstairs.

El came to the door of my room and hovered, one foot in front, invading my air space.

'Watch it!' I said.

She wiggled her foot.

'Out!'

Not letting my sister in my room might seem mean, but ...

Before I learnt to logout whenever I was more than an arm's length away from my devices, she regularly wrote things on my Facebook page that little girls think are funny like:

Dan Langley loves the Ninky Nonk

Dan Langley farted

She also regularly raided my stash of Lindor chocolate truffles and left only wrappers. A double crime because she denied it every time until I presented her with evidence from my phone, cable-tied in position to capture anyone approaching my desk.

As if I needed any more ammunition, this time she

reached for a discarded sock and blew her nose on it.

'That's disgusting.'

'It's washing,' she said.

'Washing powder isn't as powerful as your snot, El.'

In one seamless move I leapt out of my computer chair, dived like the England goalie (whoever he is) across my rug and landed at her feet. She squealed, and stepped back over the threshold.

I think she likes being banned. It gives her kudos. She tells everyone and then grins like she's won a rosette for best pony.

I followed her downstairs.

'It's stir fry,' said Mum.

During dinner Dad had a rant about the proposed changes to the benefit system. 'Every time some Eton toff says "hard-working families", the people that rely on the state to see them through get another kick in the teeth.'

Mum shared her latest birthing drama from the hospital. 'Honestly, if I get another shoulder dystocia this week I'm going to have a breakdown.' Dystocia means stuck – it's an emergency but usually turns out all right. Mum's the most experienced midwife there so she gets the tricky cases. If ever she has a baby that *doesn't* make it, *she* doesn't make it to the tea table.

The next topic was El's homework – draw a balanced meal. I helped out by building a food tower – an apple on top of a fruit scone on top of malt loaf on top of an orange juice carton. Ta-da!

'No one likes a smart arse, Dan,' said Dad.

He was too late, El was sold on the idea.

What we didn't discuss was *the visit*. I was playing the verbal version of if-I-can't-see-you-you're-not-there. Unfortunately Dad wasn't. He was just waiting for the right moment. *Never*.

'We'll have pudding when we get back,' he said to Mum.

'Come on, Dan,' he said to me. 'Let's go and see if we can wake up that friend of yours.'

I followed him out to the car. He hit the key fob and as the doors unlocked the mirrors folded out. Smooth!

It took twenty minutes to get to Frenchay Hospital. Not long enough to prepare yourself. We parked and paid two pounds fifty. Rip off!

'You all right?' said Dad.

'Fine,' I said.

Anything but.

Forty minutes later we were back in the car and I had post-traumatic stress disorder.

We'd got there to find Ty's dad in the corridor, looking grey – and I don't mean the hair. He shook our hands and went for a cup of tea in the canteen.

We rang the bell and a nurse came to let us in.

Dad sat by Ty. I sat at the end, near his feet, already freaked out. I concentrated on breathing, and not blubbing. I don't know what I looked like but my face felt as though it belonged to a Ken doll (but less expressive). The ward was like *Casualty* – wires, bleeping, red lights, white sheets, grey metal bed, grey floor, uncomfortable chair. It wasn't like the maternity hospital, which has rooms decorated like bedrooms. But that's for the beginning of life, not the end.

Trash that thought.

Dad took Ty's hand.

'Rotten bit of luck, Ty. But I know you're going to be fine. That head of yours needs some time out to get better but a day or two and you'll be up and about. If anyone can brush off a spat with a white van, it's you. I remember when . . .'

Every so often he turned to me and smiled. Waited to see if I was going to speak . . .

When I didn't, he patted my knee with his free hand and on he went, steady pace, telling a few stories about us as kids . . .

'Buzz Lightyear and Woody! You two insisted, even though it was Halloween . . . had a full-on scrap in the playground with a pumpkin.'

Ty didn't flinch, twitch, open an eye. When the blind panic subsided, leaving only normal panic, I studied him. He was breathing with a respirator and had a heart monitor and a tube for his pee and a drip in his arm. There was a gash above his eye but no other signs of violence. I couldn't believe he could hear Dad wittering on, he was too . . . flat-looking. The idea that he might be already dead, his soul gone, his dreams of doing surgery on other people's heads over, made me gag a bit on my own spit. I saw the sheep's eye, wondered what they do with human eyes in a post-mortem, pushed the thoughts away. Dad droned on.

'Don't get too comfortable in that bed, Ty. Your mum relies on you to keep those brothers of yours in line ...'

A rush of air and fast footsteps announced the arrival of a nurse.

'Time for his obs,' she said, like they were dog treats.

I moved out of her way, grateful for an excuse to get up, and, because I didn't want to look at Ty any more, I kept on walking. Through the double doors, along the corridor, back towards the main entrance. If Dad called after me, I didn't hear him.

Finally outside, I leant against the wall, next to the bandaged and slippered patients who were enjoying an after-dinner fag. I waited, trying not to breathe in their cancerous smoke.

'Don't worry about it,' said Dad as he came out. 'It's not easy seeing a friend in that state. You came, that's what matters.'

Dad was right. It wasn't easy. And neither was getting access to a satellite, but it was worth a try. What if Ty ended up needing twenty-four-hour care? That would cost money. The van driver needed to pay for what he'd done. That's why I settled in for an all-nighter with Red Bull and Dairy Milk. That, and the fact that I didn't trust myself to sleep. Who knew what nightmares having a brain-dead friend would bring?

One thing that was clear from my research was that there are zillions of satellites dotted all over the sky, controlled from loads of different locations. Somewhere, something would have been overlooked. It was a question of patience. And patience I have a lot of. All I needed was a chink in the system that would let me in. If the banks and the oil companies couldn't protect themselves from exploiters, maybe the military weren't immune either ...

Later on in my story, when my world went pear-shaped, people were astonished that I was just a kid. But the elite are all young. The internet is like playgroup, full of toys. We've grown up with it. Look around. Jonathan James, aka cOmrade, hacked the NASA computer system when he was sixteen. The Netsky and Sasser worms that infected millions of computers were written and released by a teenager. The people in authority are old and ignorant – they see code as something that has to be stuck together like Lego. They don't see what we see – that code is like clay that can be moulded, shaped, manipulated. They have no idea what time and determination can achieve. Or how to stop us.

9

I'd never gone out much, but with Ty in hospital, Soraya off with her new beau and Joe climbing the walls (ha!), there was even less reason to leave my room. Hacking a spy satellite was a challenge I wasn't prepared to fail. I was already mentally committed when it occurred to me that satellites look down, not along. No chance of reading a registration plate from above. So unless the white van that hit Ty had a massive logo on top, the task was pointless. But the task itself had become the point.

It was a laborious process – too long to measure in comedy shows. And I was getting nowhere fast. You need to understand that real-time hacking is nothing like what you see at the cinema. In a film, if a computer nerd has to crack a code to open a door or a safe, he uses a laptop to cycle through all the possible combinations and find the right one before the FBI arrives/the hero explodes/the human race ends. This is not possible. A computer takes between four days and nineteen years to crack a 128-bit encrypted code. A computer in the hands of a very clever hacker still takes between four days and nineteen years.

No surprise, then, that hackers don't bother with code breaking – they find another way in. It's like a burglar prising open a window, rather than attempting to get through the mortice lock and security chain on the front door. However, what *really* speeds up the process is to find a way round the security *and* a clue. We're talking social engineering – jargon for using the fallibility of the target being hacked. Someone once tried to do it to my gran. Luckily she has me as a grandson.

'Do you know, Dan, I had a phone call from the bank this afternoon?'

'Did you, Gran?'

'I did – some little beggar had taken money from my account, no less!'

'Are you sure?' At this point I wasn't really listening, just responding to keep Gran happy. I thought she'd bought something and forgotten about it.

'It was sorted out ever so quickly.'

'Good,' I said.

'All I had to do was confirm my details and that little number on the back of the card and he said he could sort it out and I'd get all the money back.' She smiled, pleased with the result. 'He was called Andrew.'

My head caught up with what she was saying. I got Dad, he rang the bank, and Gran got the money back even though it was her fault. Dad made her promise to never give any personal info to anyone she didn't know.

'But he was from the bank,' she said.

See? Duped by a combination of coding *and* social engineering.

(Btw, my gran's not stupid – loads of people fall for those scams.)

Anyway, if I was going to successfully hack a spy satellite *I* needed a clue. One tiny bit of help to lower the odds. And I got it, thanks to Dad.

A week and a half after Angel first suggested I infiltrate the security of the great US of A – which equates to maybe ... eighty hours of computer time – the parents arrived at the door of my room (with El listening in from hers). It seemed I'd been on their radar for a few days – evidently only so much geek behaviour could pass as normal ...

'We need to talk, Dan,' said Dad.

For a crazy moment I thought they were about to say they were getting a divorce. That was the tone.

'OK,' I said.

'It's not healthy to spend so much time on your own, darling,' said Mum.

'You need to get out,' said Dad.

Relieved that I wouldn't be the child with two bedrooms and no clean pants in either, I nodded, ready for the usual five minutes of advice before reverting to situation normal.

'You're only sixteen and we think you need some rules.'

'Like?'

'I want you downstairs in the evening after your homework and no computing late at night,' said Dad.

'OK,' I said. And then, because I seemed a bit too willing, 'But I don't see why. I'm fine.'

'You're very pale,' said Mum. 'And I think too much looking at a screen is bad for your eyes. They're slightly bloodshot.'

wink

Dad's bright idea was that I come down at nine o'clock every night and watch telly with him. Why swapping one screen with another would help, who knew? I agreed anyway. Previous experience told me no one would enforce it.

They were leaving, satisfied with our little chat, when Mum said, 'We've had a letter about the geography trip. Mr Richards says you need to go.'

'I'm not bothered,' I said. 'I can get the data off someone else, and it's quite expensive.'

'You're going,' said Dad.

Great! A bus journey to West Wales, all afternoon taking measurements of a river, sharing a room and a loo with people I hardly know from the other class, a whole day of experiments about speed of flow and direction and dead ducks and cold feet and misery, a second night away with unfunny teachers and fake teambuilding, a debrief and, eventually, home. Just what I needed.

They disappeared, but at nine o'clock El came to say

goodnight and reminded me I was expected downstairs – smug look on her face. I told her where to go but Dad started yelling at me so I gave in and trudged downstairs. Other kids row with their parents but I choose the path of least resistance and mostly things blow over. A few nights of compliance and Dad would go quiet again – I'd stake my Pay As You Go fund on it.

I didn't exactly have high hopes of my hour bonding with Dad in front of a whodunnit, but for once he let me choose so we watched a documentary about Afghanistan. It was interesting – although remind me never to respond to those ads that make the army sound like Go Ape. More importantly, it gave me a clue about where I might find a window I could prise open. Thank you, Channel 4.

Around four o'clock the next morning I had a breakthrough. I didn't need to infiltrate the Pentagon, or any other major headquarters, because a remote base station in the field near Camp Bastion let me inside the US Military network. It's complicated, but all you need to know is that I searched for big chunks of data moving between Washington IP addresses and an area of Afghanistan occupied by the Americans, identified the military set of numbers and then sent random emails until I got an out-of-office reply confirming it was a military location. Knowing the location was the 'clue'.

I got inside and started sniffing IP traffic. The NRO (National Reconnaissance Office) operates all the satellites so I scanned live video streams in and out of the Pentagon, looking for those initials. How authorities dare protest about their systems being hacked, I don't know, because that was all it took. I identified a server, found my way in, picked a random location and was rewarded by the feed from a satellite live on my screen. All I could see were fields, with the time, date, co-ordinates and other stuff that I didn't understand superimposed – but that wasn't the point. I cracked it – *that* was the point.

10

I went to school the day after my moderately impressive hack and walked home with Joe.

'Not going to the climbing centre tonight?'

'I've strained my wrist,' he said. 'Might take two weeks to get better.'

'Bad luck.'

He nodded.

'Did you go and see Ty yesterday?' I asked.

'Yep. Nothing changes.'

'Do you think he's still there?'

'Of course, idiot.'

'How do you know?'

'He's still breathing. I think that's the usual way of telling.'

'You know what I mean,' I said, a bit irritated by Joe's blind faith.

My message alert went off. A short burst of Darth Vader – sad but true. I took it out of my pocket and yelped. Seriously, I yelped.

Ty is awake and talking. He's going to be fine. Love Mum x

'He's more than breathing,' I said, showing Joe the text.

Joe flung his arms round me and I slapped mine round him, which was odd but good. It wasn't like I'd been worrying about Ty *all* the time, but knowing I didn't have to was a big relief.

'Shall we go and see him?' said Joe.

I hesitated, because I was keen to get home and have a proper play with the US reconnaissance satellites. Before breakfast I'd mapped the controls onto my phone so I could manipulate the camera, but had only managed to follow New Yorkers jogging through Central Park before Mum shooed me off to school. I didn't even know if American satellites were trained on South West England but that was my next step, just in case the evil van did have some markings I could see.

Anyway, after some mental wrestling I made the right decision. I figured stalking the planet could wait. I texted Mum to tell her what I was doing and we caught two buses to the hospital – same route I used to take to see Grandad.

'Do you remember anything?' I asked him.

'I'm called Milly. And I live on a cloud,' he said. Dreamy voice. Googly eyes.

I started laughing but Joe looked terrified, which made Ty laugh. Good to see.

Talk about 'off' and 'on' switches! Ty had been 'off' for thirteen days. But he was totally back 'on'. His blond

Tintin quiff was restored, his light blue eyes were open, they'd taken away all the beepy stuff and the cut on his head was just a red line.

'Are you completely better?' asked Joe, clearly freaked by Ty's little joke.

'If I could pee, I would be.'

'You're kidding?' said Joe, looking traumatised *again*. He really needed a sense of humour overhaul.

'I wish I was.'

Joe's eyes flicked to halfway down the bed sheet. It was too funny for words – he clearly thought the accident had damaged Ty's 'equipment'.

'Happens to women if they have an epidural when they're giving birth,' I said. Was there no end to my knowledge?

'They said it's because of the catheter,' said Ty. 'My brain has forgotten how to tell the muscles to let go. Or my muscles have forgotten how to respond. Either way, they won't let me out till I pee.'

'Come on, then,' I said.

Joe protested, worried that Ty shouldn't get out of bed, keen to call a nurse, but I knew what to do thanks to Mum's dinnertime tales from the maternity ward.

I turned all six taps, hot and cold, on full and let the water run down the plughole. Ty got the idea and stood at the urinal, staring down.

'Not even a dribble,' he said.

At the risk of my two friends thinking I was making a gay pass, I unzipped my fly, stood at the urinal next to him and peed. Joe stormed out of the loos, which started us laughing all over again, during which time Ty peed. For about ten minutes!

'Sorted,' I said to Joe as we came back out. He was leaning against the wall opposite the loos, looking cool without trying. (Think Harley from Rizzle Kicks.)

'Thank you, Dan.' Ty shook my hand, and announced his success to the nurse on our way back.

'Does that mean I can go home?' he asked.

She shook her head.

'Sorry, Ty, we need the doctor to see you before you can skedaddle, and that won't be until the morning.'

He looked really disappointed.

'It's only one more night,' I said.

'And I don't remember the others,' he said.

We stayed until his mum came. To pass the time I filled him in on my failed attempts to identify the van driver. He was horrified that I'd hacked the council cameras, and apoplectic (excellent word) when I mentioned spy satellites. It was predictable, given his attitude to the Pay As You Go episode in my life, but I'd hoped he'd see it as loyalty.

'You've crossed the line,' he said, which was a bit dramatic.

I tried to defend myself.

'I tapped a few buttons on the keyboard and it led me there. It's not like I'm planning on spying on Iran.'

'It would have been epic if you could have got the reg,' said Joe.

'Epic-ally illegal,' said Ty.

'Can you spy on whoever you like?' asked Joe, seeing possibilities for my hack.

I nodded.

'Cool.'

'Not cool, not even to catch criminals. Because *it's* criminal.' Ty was getting agitated, which probably wasn't good for him.

'Can't you see where the van went?' said Joe. 'Maybe he hit Ty and drove home. Get him that way.'

Talk about a light bulb moment.

'Don't even think about it,' said Ty, just as his mum walked in. She gave us both a hug and thanked us for being such good friends. (Secretly she thinks I'm a 'bad influence'.) (But not that secretly or I wouldn't know.)

'We'd better go,' I said.

'Have you heard of Gary McKinnon?' said Ty quietly.

Of course I had. He thought the US Government was hiding evidence of UFOs so he hacked the military computer system looking for proof and got himself arrested. So what? There are millions of hackers and Ty only knew the name of one.

11

The parents were out to suffocate me. Two nights running I'd watched telly with Dad, summoned at bang on nine o'clock, and gone to bed straight afterwards – boring programmes seemed to trigger hibernation. Or maybe it was because the alternative was staying up and trying to sew together the archive material to follow where the van went. I'd seen the collision, which, weirdly, wasn't as distressing as I'd expected. One second Ty was stationary, and the next the van had nudged him and he was on the ground, and then a person came running. That was it. All over in a second, and not a drop of blood on camera. It was tracking what happened next that wasn't going so well – too many satellites sweeping the earth.

I'd just hooked up with Angel online, when Dad appeared at the door *again* and even earlier than usual.

'As El's sleeping over at Gran's, how about a grown-ups' cinema trip?'

'I've got work to do,' I said, lying in bed with my laptop – no textbook, no exercise book, no calculator, no pen.

'Come on, Dan. Thursday's a great night to go out. Early start to the weekend,' said Dad.

Nothing I said made any difference to my cheery parents so I dragged myself downstairs and we trotted off to see a film about all the rich people living in a space station and all the poor people left behind dying of disease and dirt. They'd used that plot device where a computer deciphers the combination of a locked door in no time at all. I could point out the rest of the film's flaws, but won't – only the popcorn and bucket-size Coke were any good.

On Friday I skipped school. A reward. What for?

– for Ty finally coming home on Thursday afternoon. He kept being sick whenever he ate anything so had to stay in despite the successful peeing

– for three nights of behaving like the parents' idea of a 'normal' teenager

– and because I was determined to find the right historical recordings and see where the van went even though navigating the inter-satellite handover wasn't easy. The data files were huge and I was worried they might be erased at any moment.

I was deep in code when Angel appeared, and lured me away.

We chatted while we played *GTA V*. Thanks to our aimbots, we couldn't miss. The other players got more and more frustrated, which upped the enjoyment level.

Angel was impressed with a capital I at what I'd done:

great job KP

And chuffed that it was his comment that had made me have a go at the reconnaissance satellites in the first place:

id better watch what i say – jump in a lake – funny me!

And 'amazed' when I said I had the controls on my iPhone so I could manipulate the live feed. I don't know why – that was the easy bit.

I told him about Ty's recovery too:

he was lucky   – he said.

he was unlucky actually   – I replied.

true

And I explained the running water trick to help him pee.

LTS   – he replied. (Laughing to self, for recluses living in igloos.)

I went out before Mum and El came home, same routine as before.

'How was your day, Dan?' asked Mum as I wandered back in fifteen minutes later.

'Good. But I've got coursework to do.' The magic word. And a lie.

'That's a bit much when they know you're off on the geography trip on Sunday.'

I'd repressed all knowledge of the impending trip, even though I'd heard it mentioned around school. Some kids were actually excited!

'I'll get it done,' I said, 'but don't expect to see me apart from meals. Too much to do.'

Mum nodded, pleased with my mature attitude to work.

'I'll do your packing,' she said. 'They sent the kit list with the letter.'

'Thanks,' I said, already picturing the tidy layers, including waterproof trousers that would never get worn. I'm a jeans and hoodie sort. Blue or black. Trainers – white. Full stop. Don't care what other people wear. (Soraya's boy-band boy wears falling-down rust chinos, T-shirts with collars and Vans. It's like his sister's dressed him.)

As I was going to be out of my den for two whole days on the trip *and* had schoolwork to do, the parents relaxed the routine and left me alone. Perfect. More time to play with the network of American spy satellites. Knowing I'd be offline from Sunday helped me concentrate. Plotting the van's route by joining the feeds using GMT and GPS co-ordinates was fiddly, and took ages, but gradually I pieced it all together. When I finally saw the guilty van park, the disappointment was difficult to deal with. The driver reversed the van into a space between two other vans, in a row of fifteen identical (from above) vans, and a column of six. He got out and walked to a warehouse building near Avonmouth docks. I Googled it – a van rental place. My hopes that he'd parked on his own drive, I'd call the police anonymously from a pay phone, and he'd be arrested, were dashed.

I was gutted. He'd ended his journey in just about the most anonymous spot in the South West. I hated him even more, if that was possible.

For no reason I watched the rest of the recording, and saw men walk to and from vans, and a woman park and enter the building, and more vans and drivers come in and go out. And as watching people was weirdly compelling, I went back into the live feed and tried to track Soraya – see if she was with the 'boy'. (To be clear, I wasn't obsessed with *her*, but the task. I could have tracked our neighbour's Labrador just as happily.)

My phone was a bit small for fine control so I transferred the functions to my laptop and used the keyboard. Soraya wasn't anywhere to be seen but I had a good nose around Bishopston. Some hours went by, with a short break for chilli con carne, and another one for teeth-cleaning – dupes the parents into thinking I'm going to bed.

I was reading a thread about the developers slowing down time on *EVE* during its 'largest ever battle' when Angel joined in. I'd been thinking about hacking the website for the residential centre in the unpronounceable place in West Wales where we were going to stay and declaring it closed, or attacking the school email and cancelling the trip, so I shared my ideas with him. His reply came hurtling back:

morons like you are the reason society wants to control us, you should drown in a bog in Wales

It was clearly the wrong Angel. It's funny how complete strangers can say what the hell they like online but wouldn't do it to your face. I replied:

I have reported you to the moderator as you have explicitly threatened me with bog-drowning

I left and went in search of the right Angel, wondering why he'd chosen one of the most common handles, excluding DarkStar and Joker.

When I found him, he had another idea that could scupper my trip.

damage the power supply – he typed.

easier said than done – I replied.

are you saying KP isnt as skilled as he thinks he is

this King Penguin can't be bothered – why are you Angel?

got wings – he typed.

can you fly?

duh

The chat had hardly got going when Angel suggested we meet at IRC channel #angeldust. I was going to query it but he'd gone. Two seconds later I'd found it. Twenty minutes later I got past the virtual locked door (via a virtual window of course) and entered his private club. It was, if I'm truthful, thrilling. I was in the equivalent of a gangsters' den. (A virtual one.) (I repeat – online in your bedroom it's hard to believe you're affecting things in the *real* world.) They were elite hackers, doing stuff. Premiership level. I was careful not to act like a script kiddie. Avoided using acronyms or lame '133t sp3ak'. They made it clear – the ten other members of the closed group – that I was a visitor. Angel clarified the situation.

unless you pass a test

You'd think initiations would be too much of a cliché but clearly hackers share a mindset with street gangs. I had no idea what the geek equivalent of demanding you murder a rival gang member was . . .

like what? – I wrote.

we'll have to come up with something LTS

End of subject, because they had something else to talk about. Angel's group was building a *botnet*.

I've got 3832 bots and counting – that was Expendable.

It takes time to get enough bots to launch a DDoS (Distributed Denial of Service). It's a hacker's brute force way of paralysing a site. Anything can be taken down, from Vodafone – no top-ups, no phone buying, to Man United – no ticket sales, no new, shiny strip for your football-crazy son's birthday. Basically you get Mrs Naïve Computer User to open an attachment, like a YouTube video with the title 'The Dramatic Moment When . . .' but there's a virus in the link, or you get them to visit an infected website. Either way, hey presto, their computer is part of the botnet. Repeat this twenty thousand times and you've got yourself a decent size botnet. When the botmaster activates the virus, whatever site he's targeted goes kaput! It's the virtual equivalent of trying to get all the passengers on the *Titanic* into the lifeboats.

   You need to bring 5000 – Angel.

   I have over 5000 – Anaconda.

   good job – Angel.

   do I get my points? – Anaconda.

   yep – Angel.

   Anaconda disappeared at that point.

   Seemed like collecting 5,000 bots might be my 'initiation'.

   who's the target? – I typed.

   wait and see – Angel liked to be in control.

   It didn't stop the others discussing who deserved a DDoS. I wasn't that interested so while they dissed eBay, Facebook, Amazon, Ask.fm . . . I played a few rounds of *Counter Strike* on my computer – they've got an anti-cheat system that's fun to dodge.

   When Angel left the channel, I did too. I had a poke around GCHQ, 'Government Communications Headquarters – keeping our society safe and successful in the internet age', wondering how easy it might be to find my way inside.

   I've got no idea when I went to bed but I remember thinking, maybe for the first time, that a group of hackers could cripple anything – the National Grid, the cooling towers in a nuclear plant, air-traffic control. I should have been terrified by the prospect, but I think, if I felt anything, it was probably excitement.

12

By ten o'clock Sunday morning I was on a coach heading for a foreign country where every sentence goes up at the end. I sat on my own near the front. The back was noisy, and I wanted to sleep. It was a three-hour journey with one loo stop in the middle – that was when my peace was interrupted.

'Can I sit here?' said Ruby – a girl from the other class that I had never looked at, spoken to or sold stolen credit to.

'Sure,' I said.

'I feel a bit sick.'

I budged right over and pressed myself against the window. Just kidding!

'Don't worry, I'll aim for the aisle,' she said.

'Make sure you do.'

We sat in silence.

'Look! A red kite,' she said, leaning across me and pointing.

'Sure it's not a blackbird?' I said, squinting. That was all it took to get us chatting.

'I'm going to work outside – something to do with

wildlife, and never ever wear a suit. What about you?'

I shrugged. But as her face seemed to want an answer I said, 'Game developer, maybe.'

'You mean computer games?'

'Well, I don't mean Monopoly.'

'I like Monopoly,' she said.

We really had nothing in common. That didn't stop us talking all the way to Cardigan Bay. We covered immigration, Britain's Got Talent, coursework versus exams and favourite sandwich. (Me – bacon and cheese on white. Her – cheese, jam and lettuce. Yuck!)

Ruby was a good name for her because her hair was red, not post-box red obviously, but the colour they call red which is actually copper or maple or marmalade.

'I heard about the phone thing,' she said.

I blushed. Not because *I* cared, but because she obviously did.

'I did it to be kind,' I said, wondering why I was justifying myself. 'To start with, at any rate.'

She made a disbelieving face.

I carried on, pathetically trying to convince her that I wasn't the gangster she thought I was. (Forget Angel's den for now.)

'If you did it to be kind, why did you take a cut?'

'I had to charge for my time,' I said. I sounded vile even to myself.

'Anyway, it doesn't matter to me what you do,' she said.

I hoped that wasn't true because in the hour it took to get from Llllwyngogogcanwyn services, or whatever it was called, to the Riverside Centre, I'd fallen for her. I had two days to change her mind about me.

13

The gods were in my corner. Straight after lunch we were put into groups and yes, I was with Ruby. Even better, I had no rivals for her attention because we were with Aiden, Harry, Scarlett and Shula. Teachers are so predictable – sprinkle the idiots and terrorists in with the dull and the diligent and every group will get some sort of results and there won't be any incidents. (Bear in mind, the teachers didn't know about my extra-curricular talent – I scraped in as diligent.)

Ruby and I sorted out the work between us, and to be fair, the others were willing enough helpers, happy to not have to think. Scarlett produced the neatest table of results of all the groups although if you'd asked her she couldn't have told you what any of it meant. I tried to win Ruby over by being polite, enthusiastic, knowledgeable, funny etc. By teatime she was sick of me.

'Are you trying to impress me?' she asked as I walked with her to the girls' block.

'No,' I said, too quickly.

'Only I'd prefer it if you were normal,' she said.

'I can be that,' I said, smiling like a bad salesman.

'And not a hacker.' I didn't like the face she made. Like I was a cheese and onion burp.

'Hacker's just a word,' I said, not really knowing what I meant.

'See you.' She opened the door to her building and disappeared.

She sat at a different table from me for tea, was put in a different team for charades, and the next day all the groups had to split in two, one to experiment and the other to record observations. Some bright spark in our group decided to divide by gender. The boys got the job of wading around in the water, the girls did the timing and the distance. By lunch, Aiden, who is small and insignificant, was freezing.

'I've got another fleece if you want it.'

'Thanks, Dan,' he said.

I was going to go and get it but he tagged along.

'Do you think the results we're getting are all right?' he asked.

If I'd been with anyone else I'd have laughed. *Who cares?* But there was something about him shivering that brought out my previously unseen compassionate side.

'Yes, they're fine. The flow is bound to be faster . . .' I reeled off the basics.

He had more questions – they lasted us all the way back to the canteen so I ended up sitting on my own with him, talking geography. Yippee! Two saddos together.

'I really get it now,' he said. 'Thanks, and for this.'

He looked down at his own body, swamped by my black fleece.

'It's fine, Aiden.' It wasn't like people were queuing up to sit by me.

He was like a different person in the afternoon. Not only did he actually speak and laugh, but he volunteered for all the tasks.

'What did you do to him at lunch?' said Ruby while I was packing up the equipment.

I was going to say, 'Gave him a legal high' but managed to divert my tongue halfway through and say, 'a little help.'

Mr Richards came over and interrupted us. Damn!

'Dan, I noticed you giving Aiden a hand. Really good to see.'

He walked back to the block with me.

For the teambuilding quiz in the evening they picked the names out of a hat (except it was a bucket) – no luck there. Shame, I was hoping to build on the tiny bit of goodwill I'd detected from Ruby. Instead I concentrated on winning, which we did.

The coach ride home was my last chance. I got on early and chose a seat near the front but Ruby sat with Amelia, two seats ahead on the opposite side. I studied her (while talking to Aiden – my new BFF). It's weird what attracts you to one person and not another. She kept tucking her hair (which, unlike all the other girls', stopped at her shoulder, not her bum) behind her ear and letting it slip through her fingers, and tilting her head a lot. Her sleeves were too long – that looked cute, even though she picked her nails.

It would have been over before it had begun, but the bus arrived back as school was chucking out so I confided in Joe and Ty (who'd come in for a half day).

'No chance,' said Ty. 'She's not the sort to go out with someone like you.'

The head injury hadn't made him any nicer.

'Meaning?'

'You're bad news, Dan.'

'You could ask her to go for hot chocolate and explain,' said Joe.

'Explain that I stole lots of dosh by hacking?'

'Explain that you don't do it any more, because it was wrong. You've seen the error of your ways. You're a new, and better, version.'

As if that was going to work . . .

The next day, when I spotted Ruby in the corridor outside her classroom, I gave it a go anyway.

'Come with me for a hot chocolate after school . . . or a milkshake. I want to explain about the phone thing. Please.'

'Get lost,' said Amelia.

'I will, if Ruby tells me too.'

I wanted to make my eyes huge and sad like the cat in *Shrek* but she'd said she liked me normal so I didn't.

'All right,' she said. 'To shut you up.'

Now I wanted to make my eyes mean and squinty

to frighten Amelia, but I didn't do that either. I did, however, do an involuntary skip after I turned the corner. I was turning into someone from *Mary Poppins*.

The thing with Ruby could have saved me. I wanted to be with her. She didn't want me to be involved with anything illegal. Ergo, stop the hacking, get the girl. And that was how it was for a while. (Almost.)

14

For our first proper date we went out with the Wildlife Trust. (Yes, I became a 'friend of the planet'.)

Sunday mornings in Ruby's world meant volunteering. I wanted to see her and that was what she was doing so I went too. We all met at a courtyard on Jacobs Wells Road. It was an odd group, about twenty people, of which we were the youngest and the oldest was as old as Gandalf.

'Who's this you've brought with you, Ruby?' said an old man, who turned out to be called Ted.

'It's 'er fella,' said an old woman, name of Dot.

'Has he got a name?' said Ted.

'He's called Fella,' said Ruby.

They all laughed, and called me 'Fella' all that day (and forever after).

'When we get there, look out for the snipe and redshank,' said Ted's pal, Isaac, tapping my shoulder on the bus.

'Will do,' I said, with no idea what either of them looked like.

'Fella's got his own bird to gawp at,' said Ted, starting

a laugh that turned into a cough.

Ruby winked at me.

That day's job was on the moor, patching up the bird hide and clearing the access. I worked beside Ruby, who'd brought some gloves for both of us. She was cutting back the overgrowth and I was tidying the edge of the track.

'I like these long-handled sideways scissors,' I said.

'They're called lawn shears, Fella,' said Ted. His role seemed to be onlooker.

'We could do with one of those petrol-driven strimmers,' said Isaac.

'Don't need petrol when you've got a young 'un like that,' said Dot with a big belly laugh.

'Actually, he's solar powered,' said Ruby. 'Works fine as long as I keep him outside.'

'I thought he was a wind-up,' said Ted.

Everyone laughed again.

'Leave the lad alone,' said Isaac. 'The poor boy's not a radio, he's —'

Ruby interrupted. 'Nothing like as useful as that.'

I'm not saying it was the wittiest banter, but it was nice. They really liked her, and she liked them.

Ruby had made us a picnic – peanut butter sandwiches, salt and vinegar crisps, apples and Ribena. It was like days out with my gran and grandad, sitting in the fresh air, wrapped up warm, fiddling with sticks and chatting.

'What is it this week, then, Ruby? Black Forest gateau?' asked Ted.

'You're the wind-up merchant,' said Dot. 'You shouldn't take things for granted. She might not bring one, one day.'

Ruby had already reached into her rucksack and brought out a tupperware.

'She's a wonderful girl,' whispered Isaac. 'Always brings a cake.'

'Always a Victoria sponge,' said Ruby. 'I don't know how to make anything else.'

'You can't beat jam and cream,' said Dot.

'I didn't know you could bake,' I said.

'Nothing our Ruby can't do,' said Ted, taking a huge bite and losing most of it.

It tasted delicious. Everything did that day.

In the afternoon I helped Isaac cut back some of the trees and bushes while Ruby did some bramble bashing. She was wearing a faded grey fleece and old jeans and walking boots, but she didn't look drab because her cheeks were pink and her freckles orange and her hair shining, and her smile ...

'We're very fond of Ruby,' said Isaac.

I felt like I was talking to her dad, asking for her hand in marriage.

'I am too.'

He nodded – I think I'd passed the first test.

On the way home, listening to them all going on, I was a tiny bit flummoxed by how much I'd enjoyed the day, and how much I really did like her and how much I wanted all the oldies to like me. It wasn't a typical date, but that was the thing with Ruby. It wasn't like being with anyone else.

The first week we hung out between lessons, went to the café and ate cake after school, and, on Friday, went to the cinema. In the dark I finally got round to kissing her – it was so different from Soraya's sticky pink lips. Ruby's mouth was simply a better fit all round. She came over to my house the second week and stayed to eat, and as that went surprisingly well, she came a lot more. I went to hers once, straight from school. Never again.

Her mum came into the hall to say hello.

'You must be Dan,' she said. No handshake. No smile.

'Hello,' I said. And then, because it was a bit awkward, 'Pleased to meet you.'

'And you,' she said. Tight lips. Nasty blue dress.

She managed to look *only* at Ruby, which was clever given how close to each other we were standing, and say, 'Supper's at six-thirty so . . .'

'Dan'll be gone by then.'

Ruby turned to go up the stairs.

'Stay downstairs, please, Ruby,' she said.

Did I look like a rabid animal about to attack her daughter?

'Mum!'

Ruby's mum made a face that looked like constipation to me but presumably meant something to Ruby, who took my hand and led me into the room with the funny frosted glass door.

'Am I the first boy you've brought home?' I asked.

'Yes, and I won't be tempted again,' she said.

We watched telly, with Ruby's mum popping her head in every few minutes.

'Is she always like this?' I asked.

'You mean like a guard dog?' said Ruby, making her hands pretend to be cocked ears. That made me laugh. A lot of things she did made me laugh.

'Overprotective,' I said, trying to be diplomatic.

'Only child in a single-parent family, what hope is there?' said Ruby.

She gave me the shorthand version of how her dad ended up living in Scotland.

'... Dad couldn't breathe without asking Mum first, and she's a bit the same with me.' Ruby shrugged. 'She's basically not that happy about me seeing you.'

My mum and dad were the opposite – delighted to see me in a relationship because it meant I wasn't spending all my time in my room on my own. (Yippee – sixteen, not medicated and not a recluse.) (It also meant Dad gave up on our nine o'clock bonding sessions – more yippees.) The fact that Ruby had no piercings and wanted to work with nature was the chocolate topping on the parents' cupcake. El was pleased too, because after years of gymnastic failure, Ruby managed to teach her how to do a cartwheel. All good.

Now for the not so good.

* * *

Backtrack to the café, me trying to drink the cream-topped hot chocolate without looking silly (she had no issues with her cocoa moustache), while explaining the rise and fall of my Pay As You Go scheme. On that day, I pledged to never do *it* again, insisting I was only really interested in gaming. She seemed to believe me, and there hadn't been any cause to mention *it* since.

However, my online life carried on. The hours I put in were drastically reduced, but most nights I joined in the live messaging on IRC with Angel's mob. Later on, when men in suits asked me why, I didn't have a good reason. But they pressed me, so I said I was interested in what they were up to – that was my best answer.

Ruby didn't know and didn't ask.

All this waffle is to explain that there were a few weeks of calm before the storm. A few weeks where I was still ordinary, happy, in fact. The only incident of any relevance, that happened somewhere in the middle, was a night-time chat with Angel's crew. We were talking about my spying activity, which had included:

– people leaving the Kremlin in big coats
– drunks leaving The Cambridge Arms
– watching the queue outside the Kellaway chip shop
– Tokyo rush hour
– Arizona (the land of nothing)
– tourists at the Great Wall of China
and loads of other random locations.

Angel typed:

do something with it – don't just watch

like what? – that was me.

track a celebrity and sell the photo

catch a royal having an affair

spy on the US forces with their own cameras

hack a drone and fly it

could you do that KP? – that was Angel.

if I wanted to be blacklisted by the most powerful country on the planet I could – me.

China is most powerful

They went off in another direction, arguing about wealth, population, and the fact that all the clever kids are Chinese. I followed the chat while playing *Counter Strike* on my laptop. It took an unexpected turn.

thats your challenge KP – hack a drone – typed Angel.

He went offline, and so did I. But his words stayed on my mind.

15

Ruby had Duke of Edinburgh expedition training, leaving Saturday morning and getting back late Sunday. (I wished I'd signed up. Knowing she'd be with Ty made me feel left out – very childish.) She couldn't even come over on Friday night because she was having a takeaway with her mum, so after school I sat in the kitchen for a bit, eating Wagon Wheels – El's favourite – a bit aimless.

'Will you help me build a Tudor house?' she said to Mum.

'I'm on lates tonight and tomorrow, and look at all this.' Mum spread her arms out to imply mess. 'Maybe Dan could help?'

Out of character, but I said, 'All right.'

I made El sketch her ideal Tudor residence while I rummaged through the recycling. An hour later we had a house-shaped black and grey model made from inside-out cereal boxes, electrical tape, kindling and toothpicks.

It was 5.32 p.m. and I had nothing to do all weekend, unless I went volunteering without Ruby on Sunday, which I thought I might. Could talk about her even if

I couldn't talk to her. (Meet Dan, the lovesick puppy.)

I don't do boredom, so no surprise that my thoughts wandered in a particular direction.

Hacking a drone – was it possible?

I tidied the crap off my desk, in preparation.

As I'd already breached the US Military's network to hack the spy satellite, an American drone was the obvious target. I had the first, and maybe most difficult, step in my pocket. The question was whether a camera with wings was any more complicated to access and hijack than a satellite camera?

I settled down to some research.

Drones (flying robots, pilotless planes, UAVs) are everywhere. The army has them, Japanese farmers have them (for crop-spraying) and so do wildlife enthusiasts (to track endangered species like cheetahs). They're used to hunt hurricanes and to find people that have fallen off mountains in the Rockies. Drones are cool. Low-level flying, eyes, ears, weapons – what's not to like? The US has Predator drones that fly over Afghanistan, Iraq, Somalia – places like that – looking for terrorists they can lob a missile at. They get it wrong quite a lot of the time and kill random locals, but as the controllers flying the drones are safely on US soil, in the desert in Nevada, nothing happens. The UK has Reapers doing something similar but evidently we only hit terrorists (either that or we're better at lying).

I got inside the US Military network through the base station in Afghanistan, like before, and poked around.

You'll probably be able to sleep easier at night when I tell you that, despite my expertise, accessing a drone wasn't as simple as finding the video feeds. I couldn't tell which servers might be responsible, and there were plenty of them. All very time-consuming. There was nothing to report for thirty-six hours except that I ate spaghetti Bolognese, Shreddies, a ham sandwich, fish pie and chocolate fudge cake and slept twice for short periods. At various times I tracked Ruby. Before you jump to conclusions, *not* by hacking, but by using Find My Friends on my iPhone – a clever little app that she had accepted my request to join.

Early Sunday morning, Reuters reported that the Americans were flying surveillance drones out of a base in Djibouti to spy on the Somalis. I found a busy server with lots of repeats of activity where the drones were supposed to be in operation. It felt right, and was begging to be breached. I got inside, tried a few things and, without too much trouble, took charge of a surveillance drone. My screen showed a head-up display – data superimposed on a grainy aerial image of a building, co-ordinates, headers, stuff – not wildly different from the screens you get on Xbox, which seemed wrong on some level. I checked to see if my controls worked – they did . . . and gave the drone straight back, but for those few seconds the pilot on the ground lost the upper hand. It was a rush. You don't need to take drugs to get one. Hijacking part of the world's greatest power's defence system works just as well.

16

I woke up way too late (noon) to go volunteering. Not that it mattered. I was more interested in hooking up with Angel and 'mentioning' the fact that KP had successfully hacked a drone. It was funny how he was as much one of my friends as Joe and Ty, even though we'd never eyeballed each other.

Sadly, the cheery parents upset my plan.

'Up you get, Dan. We're going out for Sunday lunch.'

Mother's Day, Father's Day, and other occasions are celebrated in The Cambridge Arms – end of our road, turn right, which is handy if the parents have one too many!

I dragged myself out of bed, showered (which was overdue – there's something about the adrenalin involved in coding that makes you smell bad), ate a banana, found time (before the hollering started) to locate Angel in the worldwide wilderness and send him the lines of code to prove my superiority. I was already looking forward to being a fully qualified member of whatever 'gang' it was he was head of.

Off we went.

It was quite bright outside and I made the mistake of squinting to limit the amount of Vitamin D I got in one shot.

'You need to get out at least once a day, Dan,' said Dad, helpfully.

I nodded. Usual strategy.

'Have you started revising yet?' asked Mum, a little wary. She tries not to put any pressure on. Children are sensitive souls, evidently.

'They've said Easter will be soon enough.'

'That's only two weeks away,' said Dad, King of the Calendar. I resisted the urge to clarify that the Easter holidays were two weeks away but the Christian festival known as Easter was four weeks away.

'What are you going to have?' said El.

'Gammon, egg and chips,' I said. 'And I'm not sharing.'

El always has a roast but her greed for chips overcomes her.

'Ten is a lot of subjects to get through,' said Mum. 'Maybe you should start doing a bit after school . . .'

I went along with the parents' advice and pretended to be considering which AS-levels to take. At some point in the meal they dared to say the word 'university' – hoping I was going to be the first one in the family to go.

'That's the plan,' I said.

'You come out with a big loan, so it's best to choose a subject with a chance of a job,' said Dad.

'Or I could never work and never pay it back,' I said.

I scraped the last bit of sticky toffee pudding off my plate, took a tiny bit of El's and told them I was off to see Joe, leaving her with her tongue stuck out and Dad telling her to behave.

Joe was in, which was good. Joe's parents were out – even better. Joe was playing a shoot-'em-up I didn't recognise – interesting. On his ceiling – awesome.

'When did this happen?'

'Set it up yesterday. It's heaven.'

The room was dark but Joe's smile beamed through regardless, powered by happiness. He was reclining on a beanbag, using the whole ceiling as his screen. Further inspection revealed a projector balancing on its end, supported by cushions.

'Where did this come from?'

'School. I borrowed it for the weekend.'

I didn't interrogate the legitimacy of the 'borrowing'.

'Brilliant idea.'

'Not mine. I saw it on YouTube.'

I took up my position on the second beanbag and started annihilating anything that moved. In between the sort of shouting you can only enjoy when you have the house – and ideally street – to yourself, we talked about Ty's occasional memory problems (that seemed to occur at handy moments), and the climbing centre (Joe had entered a bouldering competition), and exams (Joe said his parents hadn't realised when they were yet), and Ruby (not a patch on Soraya to look at, according to Joe). And then the conversation turned again.

'Did you ever manage to see what happened to that van that hit Ty?'

I told him about the graveyard of white vans.

'Took me ages,' I said. 'Couldn't believe it when I saw him park ...' I shook my head, still angry that I'd wasted so much time chasing a loser that randomly ran over cyclists.

'*I* can't believe you know how to do that stuff,' said Joe.

'I don't "know", I work it out. Like you work out how to scramble up a wall defying gravity, gecko-boy.'

He put his legs in the air, which looked pretty funny, like a baby having its nappy changed.

'Hacked anything else, then?'

I should have kept schtum. But how was I to know that the friend who had bought stolen credit and applauded my attempt to track the van would freak out at a drone?

'You're kidding, right?' He put his legs down and sat up, missed three easy targets that I got in three shots. Then got himself killed.

While I waited for him to respawn, he said it again.

'You're kidding, Dan?'

'No,' I said, concentrating on the action. 'It was a bet, that's all.'

Next thing I knew he'd grabbed my controller but I didn't let go, so we had a kind of scuffle. Dim I might be, but I really thought we were messing, till he put his foot on where my six-pack would be if I had one.

'What the hell?'

'Look at me,' he said, which immediately tripled my annoyance because when I was in my ADHD period Mum and Dad were forever taking my face in their hands to make sure I was listening.

'It's no big deal. It's just typing,' I said, still flat on the floor, which is a bad position if you're trying to defend yourself.

'Tell me you didn't hack a drone, Dan!'

'Can you lay off the high and mighty, Joe? And get your foot off.' I pushed him off and sat up.

'You need to get rid of it, the code or whatever it is.'

'*OK!*' I said, keen for him to calm down. 'Can we carry on now?'

He didn't answer so I lay back down and carried on shooting but with eagle eyes staring at me with no intention of playing, it was no fun. It took him a few minutes but when he finally spoke he'd thought of some tricky questions.

'Whose bet was it?'

'Someone I know.'

'What have you done with it?'

'What?' Pretend innocence.

'The code. Did you give it to someone?'

If I'd used the tactic I employ with Dad I'd have carried on denying any guilt, and waited for him to get over himself, but he wasn't my dad. He was *meant* to be my friend. And I didn't like the way he was looking at me.

'What if I did?'

Ballistic – that's the word. He got up and pulled the plug out of the wall. Turned on the light. Shut the door. And stood in front of it, arms folded. The climbing had changed the shape of him – he looked strong, dark brown biceps bulging out of the sleeves of his white T-shirt.

He shouted, 'You gave someone you don't know —'

'I know Angel —'

'You gave someone you couldn't recognise in the street the controls of a US drone. A lethal weapon that could strike anyone ... anywhere ...'

'You can make it sound that way if you want, but it was just an initiation. A test. And no one's going to bomb anything, because it was a *sur-veill-ance* drone.'

'You've been played, Dan.'

17

Ten minutes after Joe gave his verdict on my spectacular hack, I was on my way home. There was no telling how long it would take him to calm down.

I let myself in. The rest of them were back from the pub, but I shot straight upstairs and went online to try and find Angel. There was no sign of him. It didn't mean anything. He *was* allowed another life away from the keyboard.

I tried on and off all through the rest of the day. There'd been whole days, and longer, between meets before. It didn't mean anything. But in the back of my head (and quite often right in the front) there was doubt. Doubt wasn't something I'd had a lot of experience of – and I didn't like it. Apart from anything else, it made me have conversations with myself, which was pointless – and mad.

Dan: It was a random decision to ask me to hack a drone, because we were talking about spying.

Dan: I agree, it was a challenge based on the fact that I'd already hacked the spy satellite.

Dan: Unless Angel saw an opportunity in between the chat to slide it in?

Dan: Or did Angel get the idea there and then?

Dan: Is Angel a kid, or an adult?

Dan: He talked like a kid, no punctuation.

Dan: Surely this whole thing can't hang on full stops.

Dan: Obviously not.

Dan: Stop stressing about it.

Dan: I will, as soon as Angel's back online.

Dan: Joe could have a point – I have no idea who Angel really is, he could be a psycho.

Dan: If you want to fly a drone it's a bit random to roam around the internet, stumbling upon people that you hope might help.

Dan: Angel could do it himself – he's elite in his own right.

Dan: Exactly.

That shut all the Dans up for a bit.

But no matter how much I wanted to dismiss Joe's fears, I was spooked. So spooked I didn't even go and meet Ruby off the bus which I intended to do. If she saw my face, I was sure she'd know I'd lied. I wanted to eat Victoria sponge with her and not be a hacker. That was the first time I ever felt a second of guilt, regret, conscience. Seriously, it was the first time.

18

Angel had disappeared. There were various Angels bobbing about in the cloud but not the Angel I knew.

Life tick-tocked on. All our lessons were about preparing for GCSEs. Every night I went somewhere with Ruby after school and pretended to be normal (and occasionally forgot I wasn't) and then went home and searched for Angel. The IRC channel where his cronies hung out was vacant, hollow, abandoned. There had to be a reason – one that wasn't to do with my few little lines of passably clever (but possibly utterly irresponsible) code.

The explanations I came up with for his vanishing act were:

– his parents had caught him and banned him from using the computer

– he was dead.

Other less likely scenarios were:

– he'd got a paralysing disease (a variation on dead)

– he'd won the Lottery and gone to that hotel in Dubai with the huge water park

– he'd respawned under another handle ... like Devil or Phoenix or (please no) Predator.

* * *

'You all right?' said Ruby, after school in the café.

'Fine,' I answered, taking a glug of hot chocolate before it was cool enough and grimacing. 'Burned my tongue.'

'I might have a cure for that,' she said, leaning over and kissing me.

It was exactly a month since we'd first gone there for me to confess about my evil past and convince her it was all behind me. And five days since I'd last heard from Angel. And five days since Joe had spoken to me. (At least he hadn't told Ty.) (Or maybe he had and Ty'd forgotten – sick joke.)

'Are you worried about the exams?' she asked me.

'No, I'm worried about the party. I don't know what to wear.'

She laughed. I banished Angel from my mind and concentrated on being a witty and interesting boyfriend.

'You don't have to come,' she said.

Amelia's sixteenth. At her house in Cotham.

'I want to. We can smoke weed and do shots.' I was winding her up. The aftermath of Pay As You Go was the only glitch in our relationship. Ruby's friends disapproved of me. Full stop.

'I don't care what everyone else thinks,' she said, soft voice, beautiful eyes, a little clump of spots that just made her more real.

'So what *shall* I wear?' I asked. Earnest face. Frowny forehead.

'Are you serious?'

I hesitated long enough for her to be completely taken in, then flashed her a (hopefully) brilliant smile.

'Stop teasing,' she said, giving me a pretend thump.

There was no more teasing. Instead I walked her home – it took a long time.

'See you tomorrow,' she said, round the corner from her house.

I was looking forward to it, mostly because it was a big chunk of time to be with Ruby. Shame it didn't work out that well.

19

Parties are overrated.

This is what happens at a typical Year Eleven gathering at someone's home:

- parents do not provide alcohol
- people bring alcohol
- people bring weed
- people may bring other drugs
- parents stay upstairs
- people get drunk
- people get stoned
- people are sick
- people snog
- people who are drunk become obnoxious. And pick on people they don't like that they're too scared to pick on normally.

'You shouldn't hang around with him, Ruby,' said a little twit in our year, weaving from side to side, his eyes lagging behind like bad dubbing.

'Who asked you?' said Ruby.

'He's bad news,' he said, meaning me.

Other little twits gathered behind the weaving twit.

'We could report you to the police,' said a voice at the back.

'Go away,' I said. 'And pick on someone your own size.'

It helped that I was taller, and not drunk, and not stoned, and not an idiot.

'Think you're something, don't you?' said the weaving twit.

'Come on, Dan,' said Ruby, tugging my sleeve, 'let's go inside.'

We were out on the steps at the front, where we'd spent most of the party. Ruby was obviously thinking that inside we might find friends, or maybe parents. Don't know. Because I wasn't about to walk away from a few shrimps. And I didn't have to, because first little twit, pumped up by vodka and Red Bull or some other make-me-a-maniac-with-zero-judgement drink, took a swipe at me. Now, I'm not a kick-your-head-in type, as I've already explained, but he'd wound me up, and he was such a pathetic sight in his skinny trousers and red Converse, that I decked him. No other word for it.

Just his mates to go, I thought. Seriously, I did. Looking back it was a weird moment – like I was Jason Statham, destined to be able to single-handedly crush a dozen would-be attackers. But, next thing I knew, real life took over and I had a bloody nose, Ruby was shouting, a load of bystanders had joined in and, for the first time in my life, I was in a brawl. A proper no-one-knows-who's-hitting-who brawl. The outcome of which was that

Amelia's parents overreacted and called the police, and everyone else either called their parents (the goodies) or scarpered (this group included me, Ruby and Joe). (Ty doesn't do parties.)

'Got a death wish?' said Joe.

'It wasn't his fault,' said Ruby.

'Nothing ever is,' said Joe.

I glared at him, terrified that he was about to tell Ruby about the drone.

'That's not nice,' said Ruby. 'You're meant to be his friend, Joe.'

Joe made a noise reminiscent of a horse. As we tramped along the streets in the rain towards Ruby's, Joe gradually gave up the angry-man stuff because he wanted to hear all about the fight.

'Wish I'd been there at the start,' he said.

'Don't be a jerk,' said Ruby.

We stopped round the corner from her house, as always. She pecked me on the cheek and we watched her go, waiting a few minutes till she texted to say she was safe inside.

'We might be talking again,' said Joe, 'but you're still way out of line.'

'Maybe you're right,' I said. 'Maybe Angel played me. But it's over. I'm not doing anything like that again. OK?'

'You'd better mean it, Dan.' He looked pretty menacing under the streetlight.

'I do.' And I did.

'OK. Look, you'd better come back to mine,' he said.

'If your mum sees you she'll flip.'

'That bad?'

He nodded, a small grin slipping onto his face.

Back at his, he got some antiseptic wipes from a medicine cupboard (in our house the drugs mingle with the groceries, waiting to be overdosed on) and cleaned up my face. It was sore one side of my mouth and under one eye.

'You'll do,' he said eventually. 'But I think you'd better stay here. Mum and Dad won't even know – Saturday night's vodka night.'

'No, I'm good,' I said, still, despite everything, keen to go and check online for Angel. Totally feasible that he'd been to a grandparent's funeral on a Scottish isle with zero internet and just got back ...

'Stay here, Dan. You might have concussion ... or something.'

I caved and texted Mum, knowing she'd be asleep but would get it in the morning. I was dropping off, tired and looking forward to oblivion when Joe said, 'Is it really over? The illegal stuff?'

'Yes,' I said, loud and clear.

20

Joe came home with me in the morning. It was a stroke of genius. With my steady and responsible friend by my side declaring my innocence, any possible blame was kiboshed.

'I think you need stitches,' said El.

'You wish,' I said.

'Actually a steri-strip might be an idea,' said Mum, rifling between the pasta and the self-raising flour.

'I'll be off,' said Joe.

'Going climbing?' I asked.

He nodded. 'Got to keep in training if I'm going to get anywhere in the competition.'

Mum and Dad asked him a few questions, clearly impressed.

I finally made it out of the kitchen, intending to go online as normal, but Ty Skyped me to see how I was and remind me that I hadn't handed in the last chemistry homework, so I chatted to him for a bit. He wanted all the news from the party. I was in the spotlight again, like it or not.

I spent the rest of the afternoon lying on my bed,

half dozing, half going over the chats I'd had with Angel, trying to remember anything that might help me find him. I wished I'd gone volunteering but it was too late by the time Joe and I'd got up. Ruby'd texted me anyway and said she'd come round afterwards.

I replayed the conversation that had led to Angel issuing the challenge. Was it a whim, like I thought, or part of a grand and complicated plan? I remembered explaining how I'd mapped the controls for a satellite camera so I could move it about, and being surprised when Angel was impressed because everyone knows that's easy. So maybe I was wrong about him being an elite ... Maybe he was just a script kiddie ... He'd never shared code with me ...

The more I thought about it, the more sense it made. He was probably twelve years old, and just using other people's exploits to make a name for himself. Ha! Like I said, there are different types of clever, and chances were Angel was clever at using people. I concluded, once and for all, that Angel never expected me to hack a drone, was surprised when I did, hell, maybe even scared, and definitely wasn't going to do it himself, just wanted to blag about it.

By the time Ruby came round I was more cheerful than I had been for a week. I'd even done the chemistry homework.

And then she dumped me.

21

Ruby's mum had found blood on her shirt. My blood, or maybe one of the twits'. Ruby's mum had called Amelia's mum and got a high-frame-rate version including the fight, the police, the damage, the weed, the booze, the vomit. Marvellous. I was firmly on the guard dog's blacklist.

Ruby said she didn't want to sneak around behind her mum's back and it was an important time with exams coming up and, although she really liked me, she didn't like the Dan that sold stolen credit, and somewhere inside I was that Dan too. She said she was sorry. She looked sorry. She looked gorgeous as well. The red hair behind her ears as always, a bright green woolly scarf, rosy cheeks.

I wasn't cross. Because I decided as soon as I heard the words that I wasn't going along with it. It wasn't like when Soraya did it. The thing with Soraya was about being with a 'girl' and all I felt when I saw her with the *X-Factor* boy was miffed. Ruby was like a friend that I wanted to spend all my time with (*and* do the other stuff), and if Ruby arrived the next day arm in arm with someone else I'd hate it. HATE it. So, somehow or other, I was getting her back.

'Just going round to Ty's,' I shouted.

'I thought Ruby was here,' said Dad from the armchair.

'She had to go. See you.'

I ran, but stopped after about a hundred metres because I was out of breath. A sixteen-year-old boy should probably be able to run without chest pain. Never mind.

Ty's house is like the council tip. His dad collects everything – tyres, pallets, metal anything, plastic plant pots in their thousands (stored in leaning towers), trolleys, barbecues ...

Ty's dad's head appeared from behind a pile.

'Hello, Dan, just sorting out a few things.' He knows everyone jokes about his hoarding. 'In you go. And try not to walk into any more doors.' That was a joke about my face.

I pushed open the front door, shouted, 'Hello,' in case anyone was downstairs but went up anyway. Ty had his head in a chemistry book.

'You don't look that bad considering.'

'I can't smile,' I said, demonstrating the lack of movement one side of my mouth.

He laughed.

'You look like a ventriloquist's dummy.'

'Cheers.'

'Hope she's worth it.'

'She chucked me actually, that's why I'm here.'

'I'm not going out with you,' he said, backing away.

'Neither, but you're Einstein and I'm starting again and I've only got a few weeks to get better results than you.'

'What are you talking about, Dan?'

'I'm reinventing myself. Ruby doesn't want a scumbag boyfriend, so he's history and I'm going to work and get good results. But I'm behind so you're my tutor.'

'Are you serious?'

'Absolutely.'

He budged up and we got on with it. He had a system going – read all about the topic, answer the questions in the book, sift through the past papers (all printed off ready), answer all the questions on that topic, check the mark scheme. He knew way more than me but I could see that a few days (or weeks) with Ty and some serious effort and I'd be clutching a fistful of As like him.

When we'd done valences, limestone and mole calculations, he allowed us a break.

'Do you feel OK?' I asked. I was on his bed. He was on the desk chair. It had occurred to me that the rigorous revision system was to make up for his brain being shaken.

'You mean my head?'

I nodded.

'Mostly. Get a few headaches.'

'Do you remember anything about it?'

He shook his head. The scar was only just visible

above his eyebrow now.

'Did you really track the van that hit me?' he asked.

'Yes, but it parked in between hundreds of other white vans at a rental place.'

'Thanks anyway.'

I paused. Not like Ty to condone illegal activities.

'You wouldn't be thanking a member of "the criminal underclass"?'

'That was the old you,' he said.

I walked home feeling surprisingly good given that I was newly single and wounded. It was five and a half weeks till my first exam. I was going to surprise everyone by getting the sort of grades that make people hate you (more). I could see myself in sixth form, spending my free periods with Ruby – Pay As You Go forgotten, personal statement riddled with noble acts of volunteering and other interests (TBA), bright future guaranteed.

The feeling lasted all week. I caught up on my homework, sat at the front in classes, went to the revision sessions at lunchtime, taught Aiden – who'd developed a crush on me – the whole geography syllabus in the gaps, and studied with Ty in the evenings. I nearly made a timetable, but there are limits! Everyone noticed, from my teachers to my parents to El, who declared me a nerd.

On Friday, the last day of term, Ruby agreed to go to the café with me.

'Just friends?' she said.

'That's your call,' I said.

'Don't make it difficult, Dan.'

'I'm not. I meant that I'm here, waiting . . . working, in fact, so when you decide I *am* perfect boyfriend material, just say.'

I flashed her a huge smile. Not hard to do.

She thumped my arm, and I grabbed her hand on its way back and we walked along like that. Nothing else happened, but I'm a patient sort. And anyway, I had no time for girls – there were Newton's Laws of Motion to nail.

I strolled home, full of hot chocolate and brownie, looking forward to a couple of weeks off school, and sure of my plan to win back Ruby. The contentment was brief. The butterfly effect was about to produce devastating news. I had fifteen hours until meltdown.

22

Saturday morning. No need to get up. No need to get up for seventeen days. I opened my eyes, noted the sunlight streaming in through the gap in my blue checked curtains, thought for a while. Random . . . nothing . . . scattered . . .

Get up, Dan. Work to do.

I poured the milk up to the rim of my bowl and dropped in one Weetabix – no splash. I ate it quickly and then dropped in a second. This carried on until the milk to whole-wheat ratio resulted in a dry bowl. Very satisfying. I shoved my glass, bowl and spoon in the dishwasher and went upstairs. Everything nice and normal.

I logged onto Facebook, which I detest, but had started using to promote my new image (to Ruby) through deadly dull exam-based updates like:

is trigonometry any use in the real world?

And:

the environment is always the answer to the animal studies question

They were designed to demonstrate that I was working, whilst not being so goody-goody that they looked fake. All part of the plan to turn Hacker Boy into Keener.

That's the thing with my 'condition', if I have one. I decide things and then persevere until they happen. Time isn't a significant factor, neither are obstacles. It's key for a hacker, because coding is full of blind alleys and dead ends. I'm obsessive, I suppose, but without the anxiety and handwashing. I recommend it.

My last little ritual before I started French revision – *un moment, s'il vous plait* – was to pop onto a forum to check Angel hadn't reappeared.

My mind was so focused on looking for him that it took a few seconds to catch up with the chat that was going on. And a few seconds more to take it in. Too panicked to read the thread properly I joined in, asking for more information.

what drone are you talking about?   – I typed.
an unmanned US drone on ops in Germany has disappeared been off the radar for 12 hours
a l33t did it
how?   – I typed.
they thought it crashed in woods but they didnt find the hardware so now they think it was stolen and the live feed hacked

Despite the paralysis in my brain I could see how a drone, flying on automatic, could be hijacked by a hacker who could send back whatever footage he chose – like a crash.

critical stuff – hacking a feed into the US
military and walking off with a drone
is it loaded? – I typed.
armed and ready
its carrying Hellfire missiles
how do you know? – I typed.

I was willing it to just be talk – script kiddies full of hot air.

everyone knows
only a matter of time and it'll be on CNN

I stayed logged on but lay down on my bed, eyes closed, and tried to sort through the jumble of thoughts, all scary as hell, that were filling up my head. It took time, minutes, to get the told-you-so voices out of my head – Joe's 'You've been played', and Ty whispering, 'Ever heard of Gary McKinnon?' As well as the images of Afghan kids being bombed while playing in the street, me being dragged off in handcuffs and Ruby looking at me with utter loathing. Eventually I slowed down my breathing, and got things in order:

– Angel had challenged me to hack a drone

– I'd hacked a surveillance drone

– I'd sent Angel my lines of code so he could, in theory, control a drone (the 'in theory' was only in there to make me feel better)

– I didn't know whether the code could also access a combat drone

– Angel disappeared as soon as he got the code

– so did IRC channel #angeldust

   – a combat drone had disappeared from an American base in Germany

   – was it Angel?

   – who the hell *was* Angel?

For all I knew he was a forty-year-old psychopath, or a religious fundamentalist, or a schizophrenic hearing voices telling him to bomb Simon Cowell. I was fuming at the idea he'd been stringing me along, working me like a puppet. I'm not good at dealing with anger. I needed to do something.

Right.

I went back to my computer and started information-gathering. I followed any current threads that mentioned drones, half of which were about drone strikes, for and against, a quarter were about toy drones, research drones, drone capability, and the rest were about the missing one. I left messages for Angel anywhere I ever remembered meeting him. Mum called me for lunch. Lunch! There was no way I could swallow bread when I might be responsible for . . . a drone strike . . . and carnage.

There was no way round it – why steal a Predator unless you plan to use it?

'Dan! Come on, I've made sausage sandwiches for my hardworking boy.'

I went to the bathroom and splashed water on my face, took some deep breaths, stared at myself in the mirror and tried to make a normal face, worried that the feeling inside me would show on the outside. Fear.

Dread. Disgust. Terror. Guilt.

'Dan!'

I had to go.

'Sorry,' I said, forcing a smile as I slid into my chair and smothering my sandwich in tomato sauce to help the lumps go down.

'How's it going?' asked Mum.

'Good.'

The four of us sat round the table eating, with Radio 4 in the background. El gave a blow-by-blow account of her friend's latest YouTube video – she has her own channel called WhatBetsyDoes, full of cake-making and face-painting. I attacked the lunch as though I was ravenous, desperate to get away from the family meal.

I needed someone to talk to. Ruby was out of the question, so it was Ty or Joe. They'd both flip, but Joe would be less likely to drag me to the police station to confess. (And Ty only knew half the story.)

It might be hard to believe I ever went near a drone without thinking about what I was doing, but there's always more than one way of looking at things.

A kid kicks a football up in the air again and again, twenty ... thirty ... forty times ... desperate to keep the ball from touching the ground. A free diver holds his breath for ... twenty minutes. Actually, I've thought of a better example – there are people that can recite Pi to thousands of decimal places.

And my point is?

These things are *point-less*. Ball skills are useful but ... let it drop occasionally ... it makes no difference. Not breathing is stupid, and gives you brain damage. You can look Pi up and read it to one million digits. So why do people do these things? Answer – because they can.

To follow the argument through, a hacker might wonder whether a drone is hackable. No ulterior motive. No agenda. Simply to see if he can.

Trying to justify my actions wasn't helping. I ran faster.

Joe was on his back, shooting the ceiling, like last time.

'Stop for a bit, will you?'

'Why would I want to do that?' he said.

'Because I need to tell you something.'

I turned on the light, which took away his screen.

'Girl trouble?'

'If only.'

I told him what they were saying online. I'm not sure what reaction I expected but it wasn't laughter.

'It's not funny, Joe.'

'It is. It's funny that you think you've infiltrated the CIA or whoever owns the drones and Angel's up there flying one right now about to bomb . . . the White House.'

'He might be.'

'Dan, even if you really did get control of a drone,

like you say you did, by now they'll have patched up whatever the hole was. You're a nothing, messing about in your bedroom. This is the US Army we're talking about. If a drone's gone missing, they'll find it. You're an idiot, but that's all. Chill!'

'*You* weren't exactly "chilled" when I told you what I'd done.'

'That's because *someone* needs to try and keep you out of trouble,' he said, rolling his eyes, 'or one day you'll majorly mess up, and they'll *lock* you up. But it's not that day yet.'

I wanted to believe him. Maybe I had completely overreacted ...

'You said it was a spy drone you hacked, didn't you?' he said. 'One with a camera?'

I nodded.

'And a drone with missiles has gone missing?'

More nodding.

'Nothing to do with you, then. Come on, let's play,' he said, chucking me a controller.

I settled down on a beanbag like before and, as the action started, I felt myself relax. Joe was right. What were the chances that Angel was a terrorist? Tiny. He set me the challenge because we were talking about drones, and we were talking about drones because I'd hacked the satellite. No one made me do that. Stupid Dan. Everyone knows the internet is full of lies. There probably wasn't a Predator drone on the loose at all.

I stayed for an hour before heading home to

immerse my head in French — *bon idée*. Dad was in the kitchen, scribbling the answers in the crossword. He'd finished the Sudoku.

'Just the man I need,' he said. 'Seven across ...'

His voice was drowned by the sound of a helicopter passing over. There are often police flying about, chasing stolen cars on their way back to the Southmead Estate.

'That'll be the missing drone,' said Dad, clearly joking.

'What missing drone?' I asked, instantly sweaty.

'It was on the news.' Dad nodded towards the radio. 'The Americans have "mislaid" a Predator somewhere in Germany. The Secretary of State for Defence was on, no less. Cyber criminals, they reckon. That's the trouble with relying on technology instead of people.'

He went back to the crossword.

23

News is everywhere. I searched online sources from the BBC to Reuters, from India Today to World of Warcraft forums. I found tons of Angels, but not *the* Angel. I found people taking responsibility for the drone. I found pornography. I found lunatics demanding death to Americans, Muslims, Jews and Justin Bieber. What I didn't find was anything that shed any light on whether I was involved or not. I supposed that was a good thing. No one was shouting, 'That kid KP did it. Don't you remember? It was his challenge.' Actually, that was odd. All the other members of Angel's gang who were on IRC #angeldust knew what I knew, so where were they? The channel had disappeared, like its originator, but why weren't they roaming around trying to find me? I couldn't remember any of the handles any of them used except Expendable (because of the films) and one that was a snake like Viper or something. And, like Angel, they were nowhere to be seen. I went to look on /digi/. It's anonymous, and the content is dumped every twenty-four hours. I went fishing in the hope that someone might leak something knowing it wouldn't come back on them.

anyone seen Angel?   – I typed.

I bring you news of great joy   – someone called Dogbreath (why???).

jesus is coming

And so it went on . . .

a star in the sky

a dark star   – DarkStar (one of the many).

'We need to go,' said El, pushing my door open but staying on the landing.

'What are you talking about?' I said as I swivelled my computer chair.

She was wearing what ten-year-olds wear to parties – sparkly tights, clip-on earrings and something purple in between. A memory forced its way to the front of my brain. Mum was working because someone had called in sick, Dad had just gone to the football – I'd heard the door slam and the BMW drive away – and I was on sister duty. Today of all days.

'Where are we going?'

'Maeve's.' She read the whole invitation aloud, including the address and telephone number for RSVPs.

'OK. Give me five minutes, El.'

'I don't want to be late.'

'I don't care what you want.'

She hovered her foot, but I wasn't in the mood. I got up and slammed the door. Not shut, slammed. Babysitting! When I was on the verge of . . .

What was I on the verge of? Damn!

I scanned all the open tabs on my screen to see if there was more news, then logged out — because it's a habit. Got my Gap hoodie and opened my door, stage face on.

'OK, El. Party time!'

She didn't answer. Standard behaviour if your brother's nearly amputated your foot. I leapt down the stairs, as though being pretend-lively could help me get through my shift as 'responsible adult'.

I wasted at least five minutes looking under her bed and behind the curtains, calling, 'Come on, El. I'm sorry I was mean.'

She was nowhere to be seen, and her coat wasn't hanging by the front door. What the hell?

The level of panic was almost paralysing. Ty's accident . . . El's lack of right and left . . . the fact I was about to be held on terrorism charges. I ran. She'd never gone anywhere on her own. No way to get to Bishop Road without crossing Coldharbour Road, which is busy. Would she know to wait, or step out?

Lorries. Motorbikes. White vans . . .

It's about a mile to Bishop Road. I kept expecting to see her. How far ahead could she be? I've got long legs (but no lungs) and made it in ten minutes. I didn't know what number the party was at, because I hadn't listened properly when she said, so couldn't tell if she was already there, or already dead. It was hard to breathe, or think. Why was Bishop Road so long?

And then I saw balloons.

I rang the bell and a man came to the door. Checked shirt, monkey mask.

'I just wanted to check that El ... Elena Langley is here.'

The monkey face laughed (clearly not reading my body language). Turned and shouted, 'There's no Elena expected, is there?'

Three boys with painted faces (tiger, zebra, orange sick) ran to the door to see what was happening. Took a look and scarpered back to the animal party.

'Sorry, wrong house,' I said.

Demented, with no idea what to do, I rang Ruby. I'd repeat what I said, except it was gibberish. Luckily her answer wasn't.

'Isn't El friends with Grace? Will she be going?'

Good thinking. Grace is Amelia's little sister. Amelia is Ruby's BFF. 'Can you ring Amelia for me?'

I got off the phone and stood halfway down Bishop Road. Waiting. There was no way El could have been as quick as me. So where was she? My phone shuddered. It was Ruby ... and she had the house number.

'Thank you.'

I raced back up one block and rang the bell.

Another dad answered the door.

'I'm Elena's brother. Is she here? Only I —'

'She's not here yet,' said a girl in roughly the same clothes as El but with blonde hair, not brown. Presumably Maeve.

The mum appeared. Mums have radars that pick up distress signals.

'Is there a problem?'

I told her what had happened. (The door slamming, not the impending drone strike.)

'We should call your mum,' she said.

I shook my head. 'She's at work so she won't answer.' Not strictly true but I was still hoping for a happy, parent-free ending.

'Fair enough. Are you sure Elena knows the way?'

Stupid question. Or was it? If you're walked like a dog, or taxied about, do you take any notice of where you go?

'Actually, she might not.'

The search party consisted of me, the dad and another mum, recruited when she came to drop off. Having swapped mobile numbers, we all took different routes back to St Albans Road.

'Don't worry, lad. We'll find her,' said Maeve's dad.

I retraced my steps, which was pointless, but the party-mum had dished out the orders and mums know best. My phone went. For the first time ever, I was disappointed it was Ruby.

'Was she there?'

'No. We're out looking for her.'

'I'll come over.'

Time really did slow down. I'm serious – it wasn't my perception that was skewed, seconds dragged. I checked my phone at every other front door or shop window or driveway. A siren wailed in the distance, coming my way.

Please let it be an old man with a dodgy heart, or a baby coming out too quickly. Please let it not be a little girl, unsure of the way to a party.

The shrillness made me want to cover my ears.

The cars pulled over to let the nee-naw pass. I don't know what part of my body made the decision but I started to run, following the paramedics. The ambulance slowed at the junction and then turned left onto Coldharbour Road. I cut across the road and got honked. I turned to make an angry gesture (because I wasn't close enough to kick the bodywork) and when I turned back there was El, coming out of the corner shop.

'Where have you been?' I said, in a pretty steady voice, given that I wanted to yell *and* weep at the same time.

She held out her hand to show me the bar of Cadbury's Caramel.

'I was worried, El.'

She shrugged, and tried to walk past me.

'I'm coming too,' I said. 'I'm sorry.'

The good thing about being ten is that moods don't last long, not like teenage ones – all rage and brooding.

'There's going to be nail-painting,' she said.

'You don't have any,' I said.

'I do, I've been growing them.'

She showed me her fingers, splayed like a frog's.

There was a tiny strip of white on the tip of each nail.

'So I see.'

I kept up the jollity all the way back to Bishop Road.

'Here she is,' I said, as the party-mum opened the door.

'Thank heavens, we thought you'd gone astray. Come on in, Elena.'

El disappeared.

'I'll pick you up,' I shouted to the space she'd vacated.

'Five o'clock,' said the mum, looking behind me as though expecting to see . . .

Damn! I hadn't told the others.

'Thank you,' I said, hurrying off to text the parents still roaming the streets.

The drama had completely taken my mind off the tiny issue of a wayward drone circling above who-knew-where with a missile or two. But alone again, with nothing to do for two hours, it came back bigger and badder. I had no idea what to do. Go home and try and fix things? Bury my head in the sand pit at the park?

'Dan!' It was Ruby, striding towards me, face flushed, hair hidden in a beanie. Seeing her made it all even more desperate. She'd never forgive me if it all came out. If I *was* responsible.

'El was buying sweets,' I said.

Ruby laughed. 'Good girl,' she said.

I was torn between wanting to be left to think, and making the most of my time alone with the lovely redheaded girl standing in front of me.

'I miss you,' I said.

'Let's go and get a cake.'

We walked arm in arm down to the Gloucester Road. She'd been working all day so was keen to chat, which was good because it prevented me from blurting it all out like Confessional Tourette's — a little-known condition in which the sufferer cannot commit a misdemeanour without leaking it.

'I'm sorry about last week,' she said, as we reached the shop. 'I didn't really mean it — it's just that Mum was so cross. She worries ...'

'It's OK. I get it,' I said, taking a rogue piece of hair and putting it behind her ear. I leant across and kissed her — not a peck, a proper going-out kiss. A random passer-by clapped.

'You're not the bad guy people think you are,' she said. 'I know that.'

'Chocolate brownie or tiffin?' I asked.

It took all my willpower to park the problem and stay with Ruby, eating cake, kissing, laughing. It was nice, but a dark shadow was creeping over. I wasn't sad when it was time to get El. Ruby said she'd better get going as she was babysitting.

'Coming volunteering, Fella?'

'Try and stop me,' I said, but tomorrow seemed a long way away. I watched her walk off, battered satchel over her shoulder, before I hurried back to admire El's black fingernails, complete with white skull and crossbones.

(They're ten! What was party-mum thinking of?)

'Awesome. So how was the party?'

'Good,' said El. She was holding a party bag of monster proportions.

'What's in there?'

'A pencil with a fairy on top, a notebook, a ...'

The list went on, in between mouthfuls of miniature Curly Wurly and Cadbury's Fudge. She offered me the Crunchie.

I listened to a review of the whole party – sandwiches with crusts, not enough layers on the pass-the-parcel, scrummy cake, and made all the right noises but, inside, my mind was trying to make order out of the mess. I couldn't let the fact that I had a gift for code ruin everything.

24

There was nothing new online, or rather there was plenty of new content but it said all the same things that were already there. It didn't matter, because I'd made a decision. I could either wait and see what happened with the missing drone – that would be passive and the anticipation might kill me. Or I could find out for myself whether my little contribution to Angel's virtual toolbox in the sky was any use. I'd managed to get hold of a drone, but not one with a payload. With any luck there would be more security on something that could annihilate people praying in mosques and playing in parks. My code was probably n00b level compared to what you need to swipe the controls of a combat drone – in which case I was in the clear. Time to find out.

I went back to the base station in Afghanistan. As usual, I routed through six servers to cover my tracks – El Savador, the Maldives, Brazil, Port Talbot, and so on. There was good news and bad. The good news was that there didn't seem to be any Predators being controlled from the server I'd used to hack the spy drone. The bad news was that, without too much difficulty, I stumbled upon a parallel server, where everything looked very similar. I studied the patterns of activity over Kandahar. The chances were, based on media coverage, these drones had weapons. I chose one.

The Dan that enjoyed happy endings was hoping his way would be barred by a concept of cleverness he couldn't even recognise, yet alone sidestep. But it wasn't.

For the second time in my life I took control of a drone, except this time it was a Predator. I held in my hands the ability to target and destroy. And all Angel had to do was follow the same logic as me and he could do the same. It was terrible, like holding someone's bloody limb. I gave the control straight back, put my hands in the air and briefly considered having my first OCD hand-washing episode. I felt dirty, like I'd shown too much of myself, the hacker's equivalent of tweeting a selfie.

25

I went volunteering with Ruby. She convinced me that revision worked better if you had time away from it. I didn't take much persuading, desperate to get away from the voices in my head.

Is it Angel? Or isn't it? If it is, is he planning annihilation or having a laugh? Or is it all a coincidence, nothing to do with me or Angel? There are seven billion people on the planet. More than one must have hacked a drone ...

I was in limbo, as Gran would say, like when she was waiting for Grandad's test results to see if she should book a cruise or pick hymns for the funeral. (It was time to pick hymns.)

I met Ruby at the courtyard. It was sunny. Proper blue sky. And warm for the first time in forever. She was chatting with her geriatric fan club.

'We missed you last week, Fella,' said Ted.

'I got in a fight,' I said, because my brain was too clogged to process anything but the truth.

'Protecting your girl, were you?' he said.

'I was protecting him,' said Ruby, pretending to kick box.

'You ever get in trouble, Ruby, and you can call on me. I was trained to kill, you know.' Ted flexed his non-existent biceps.

The group all laughed. I almost did too. Being with normal (in the widest sense) people was a good idea – chase away the demons. We went in the minibus to somewhere near Chew Valley to do hedgerow management along the footpath. There were only twelve of us, much fewer than usual.

'You're quiet,' said Ruby.

'I'm at one with nature,' I said.

She nipped my arm. I feigned pain.

'What was that for?'

'Just showing how much I like you.'

'What's the next level? A slap round the face?'

'There's a willow warbler,' said Isaac, pointing.

My phone rang, sending the bird away, and probably annoying everyone. It was Joe. This was rare. FaceTime, text, Snapchat, but real-life talking – not often. I picked up.

'Have you heard?' he said.

There was a long sarcastic answer to this on the tip of my tongue. It stayed there.

'What?'

'He's threatened to bomb London.'

It's not the sort of sentence you hear every day. You'd think that would make it sink in fast, but the opposite happened with my brain. (Call it denial, I'm just telling it how it was.)

'Say again?' I said.

'The nutter that stole the drone says he's heading for London, armed and ready to fire.'

'And I'm the Green Goblin. Good one, Joe.' As I said it, I already knew it wasn't a wind-up. I made a conscious effort to stop my face acknowledging the disembowelment of my body . . . kept my voice steady.

'I'm out with Ruby, so I'll see you later.'

'You better have a good excuse, Dan, when the men in suits come. It's —'

I disconnected.

Surreal. So surreal it was film-like. There we were, a boy and his girl, with two old men, enjoying the sun on our backs as we worked to keep part of the English countryside beautiful for future generations of both people and wildlife, while far away in the capital, the population was at the mercy of a nameless evil. Surely time for Superman? The idea that I had to somehow be Superman made me catch my breath.

'What did he want?' asked Ruby, possibly not for the first time, judging by her expression.

'Wanted to know if I was going round later,' I said. In order to smile I had to jumpstart a few muscles.

'What was that thing about the Green Goblin?'

'He was in a little-known film with a spidery character —'

'OK. Don't tell me,' she said, carrying on with the hedge tidying.

I wanted to tell her. If I could have conjured a spell that guaranteed she'd stick by me . . .

'Do you think you can reach the top?' asked Isaac, as I was the only one under sixty and grazing six foot.

'I'll have a go,' I said. He passed me his long-handled shears and I trimmed the hedge all the way along, leaving Ruby to work with Ted. I was glad to be away from her all-knowing eye. It gave me a chance to get myself together.

The afternoon dragged, even the bit with cake. They all talked, and I nodded and grinned at what seemed appropriate moments. Ruby didn't press me for details until we were on the bus, homeward bound (Simon and Garfunkel – one of Dad's choices for when he's on *Desert Island Discs*).

'What did Joe say?'

No way could I tell the truth. What was the truth, anyway?

'He's worried about Ty. Says he's not getting any better. You know ... his memory and stuff?'

'I haven't noticed.'

'Yes, but you didn't really know him before.'

'I expect his mum and dad are making sure he's all right.'

It was the opening I needed. I proceeded to tell Ruby all about the rag-and-bone front garden and general lack of organisation in Ty's house.

'Shall I come to yours for a bit?' she said, as we got off the bus.

'I need to get round to Joe's. He was a bit worked up.' I sighed, as though I believed my own lie. 'When he mentioned the bouldering competition, Ty asked how long he'd been climbing.'

'That doesn't sound good.' A little frown froze on Ruby's forehead.

It felt bad, trying to get away from my best person, but I was all acted out.

'Bye.'

I kissed her, got the usual whistles from the silver-haired volunteers and ran home.

26

Social media's take on the crisis, accessed from my phone, didn't help much (and was badly written):

shoot it down POW! (On Snapchat with a picture of a pointed finger.)

he needs putting in an assylum

my aunty lives in London I dont want her to die

is this are 9/11?

got to be a hoax

we had 7/7

scared to death

As I went in the kitchen, Mum, without looking up from the sink, said, 'There's a lunatic threatening to bomb London. I've been on the phone to Uncle Rob. He says he'll stay out of the city.'

I got Dad's summary as I passed the living room. 'That cyber criminal's a bloody fanatic.'

El's question, from my doorway, was, 'Do you think he'll pick Buckingham Palace? I would.' Odd child.

I said the minimum. Like a tyre that had been pumped up too much, any more pressure – such as having a normal conversation with my family – and I'd burst. I needed to see what 'the terrorist' had to say for himself, on my own, in my room, with the door shut.

There it was, confirmed online for the world to see. An unspecified target in London would be the site of a missile hit at noon on Monday 7th April. That was tomorrow. As I read the details I did yogic breathing – one of the things Mum taught me back when I needed 'taming'. In front of my eyes, real time journalists turned the anonymous perp into Dronejacker and a celebrity cyber criminal was born. Why he picked London was the source of endless speculation. I waded through to find the original source, rather than the spin.

Did he have a lot of face or what? Dronejacker had hacked the BBC News page and delivered his message that way, dead on noon. It had been taken down but not before being screenshot and relayed by every web-watcher and news service. The words were brief, but the more I re-read them, the more I could see Angel typing them.

The US Predator drone is in London. I haven't decided where to direct the missile strike yet. How does it feel, Londoners? Knowing you might be on a job or shopping, and boom! Look to the sky at twelve noon Monday 7th April and think about all the people who are scared every day, like you are now, because of killer drones flying above them.

It's impossible to describe how I felt, so I won't bother, except to say that there was a period of mental self-harm before I picked up a pencil (presumably a deeply symbolic act rejecting my foray into cyber crime) and started to work through what I knew, and what I thought I knew, and what I thought. I followed the dominoes as they fell, one by one:

- fainting in biology
- going out with Soraya
- helping her out with credit
- word of my hack spreading throughout Dan's life and KP's
- meeting Angel online
- getting closer
- Ty having his accident
- Angel suggesting the council CCTV hack
- and then the spy satellite
- meeting Angel's 'friends'
- him challenging me to hack a drone
- sending Angel the lines of code
- Angel vanishing
- Dronejacker appearing.

That was how it looked to me, but how did it look to Angel?

I made two working assumptions. Firstly that Angel *was* Dronejacker and secondly that he wasn't a l33t grey hat, but a script kiddie with a black hat. Why involve me if he could do it himself?

So . . . Angel decides to steal a combat drone for

some crazy reason, but doesn't know how. Angel goes online and puts himself about (it's not good when you start borrowing phrases from your dad), he gets to know lots of hackers, and follows up any random chats he can turn to his advantage. In my case, Ty's accident gives him the opening to suggest a hack and see how good I am. I impress him. He gets close to me – we spend time together, gaming and chatting. I keep coming up with the goods, so he gives me the ultimate test. And I fall for it.

Whatever Angel needs he commissions – like a nifty line of code that programs the drone to take a specified route to wherever, like a fake video that convinces the American flying the thing that it's crashed.

When Angel has tricked his 'friends' into providing each element, all he has to do is put them together, and he can take control of a drone. The operators are fooled by the dummy feed and put together a search operation, but that takes a while. Meanwhile, the drone makes it to the UK. A drone is the size of a small plane. Angel hides it until he needs it – they're tricky to land so he probably keeps it flying around. They're hard to detect – that's one of the things that makes them good for spying.

All in all, good job, as he would say.

Working out that I wasn't the only mug didn't make me feel any better. We'd been socially engineered, helping Angel prise open the windows round the back of the palace while the beefeaters were manning the front gates.

So, I'd worked it out. Big deal. That left the burning question. The question I didn't dare ask myself . . . because I had no answer.

What the hell was I going to do?

27

The advice from the government department responsible for crazies that threaten the Great British Public was to keep calm. There was no evidence that Dronejacker was anything other than a delusional character taking advantage of the fact that a drone had been ambushed. There was also no evidence that the drone was even over British air space. People should carry on about their business as usual. Inspirational advice!

It wasn't working judging by the trending on Twitter of #7april and #terrorist. It wasn't working judging by the traffic cameras on the arterial roads out of London and the M25. Chock-a-block. The city was voting with its feet, or to be more exact, wheels.

I heard footsteps coming up our stairs but with my door shut there was no chance of identification. There was a knock on my door, and in the gap between the rap and a voice saying my name I had a sudden panic that it would be the police.

'Dan!'

'Come in.'

It was Ty, and behind him, Joe. It only felt marginally better than if it had been the cops.

'Let's go somewhere,' said Joe.

I thought about saying 'Walls have ears' in a hushed, spy-like tone but decided it might inflame the situation, so I grabbed a black hoodie, shouted, 'Going out for a bit,' to the house in general and trooped out of the front door. I walked in the middle, hood up, with my armed guards either side. We headed for the park.

'Joe told me,' said Ty.

'Cheers,' I said.

Ty shoved me and I stumbled. 'Shut it, Dan. He's worried, and so should you be.'

'Really?' I said, wide-eyed with pretend surprise.

'Leave it out, Dan,' said Joe.

'Explain,' said Ty, 'from the beginning.'

We sat on the roundabout, which Joe occasionally pushed with his foot to keep us slowly circling. As ordered, I went through the dominoes, and in between emphasised my complete ignorance of any sinister plot.

'If Angel had asked you to jump in a lake, would you?' said Ty, sounding like someone's mum.

Angel once typed that – it was a joke. Not so funny now.

'It doesn't matter why he did it,' said Joe, 'not now. What matters is what he does next.' A fair summary.

They both looked at me.

'Dronejacker isn't definitely Angel,' I said, half-heartedly.

'So you're not going to do anything?' said Ty. 'Just see what happens?'

He was waiting for me to declare I'd leave no stone unturned to stop the London bomber. He'd be waiting a while.

'Dan, listen, if there's enough of a chance Angel's for real, you have to confess.'

Unbelievably, Joe's word went straight through all the decision areas of my brain to its conscience. I missed a beat. Was he really suggesting I, Dan Langley, should ring ... the police, the FBI, MI5, Southmead Police Station, 101, 999, Scotland Yard, Sherlock Holmes?

'Joe's right,' said Ty. 'If you come clean they'll be much more lenient with you.'

I hadn't even considered confessing. Did that make me a psychopath, or sociopath, or plain old nutter? Causing havoc and taking no responsibility.

'No one will believe me,' I said, after a complete revolution of the roundabout. 'They'll think I'm a terrorist.'

'What's the alternative?' said Ty. I pitied his future brain-surgery patients, asked to choose between a radical life-threatening operation and a slow decline, with no sign of compassion.

'But I could end up handing myself in and finding out that I was nothing to do with any of it ... that it wasn't Angel at all.'

'And thousands of people, kids, grandmas, whatever, might die if you don't.'

'*Might*,' I said.

Their silence was more condemning than any words. I pictured my dead grandad, and Ty's great-grandma (who had whiskers like a cat) and Mandela, then Malala, the fifteen-year-old girl that got shot by the Taliban but says she doesn't hate them, and the woman coming out of the Tube station after 7/7, her face covered in white burn dressings . . .

'We'll come with you,' said Ty.

It took some time to sink in. As it did, my body sank with it. I leant back against the pole in the centre of the roundabout and let all my organs hang off my skeleton.

We circled again. The swings were to-ing and fro-ing — entertaining ghost children. The sun was setting, pinkish sky. The gate was shut, keeping out unwanted dogs, keeping in pre-school children. Not that there were any.

We circled again.

'Don't make us do it for you,' said Ty.

He was threatening me. I looked at him — a pillar of society. Neat, fair hair with the quiff just so, clever, responsible, dressed in beige chinos and a dark green jumper with a zip-neck — preppy-look, I think they call it. Even his scar was tidy. A world away from his any-old-iron dad. I switched to Joe. Cool, street, edgy. An image of myself flashed in front of my eyes — a mug shot. Words to go with it — odd, geeky, outsider.

Joe dug his heel in and we ground to a halt.

'You've got vital information,' he said. 'You *have* to give it to the police.'

A burst of Darth Vader interrupted their attempt to convince me. It was Ruby. I picked up.

'Dan, something's up, isn't it?' she said. Too much to deal with. I cut her off. Vodafone could take the blame. If Pay As You Go King turned out to be King of Drones she'd never speak to me again, anyway.

'So ...?' Ty was staring at me.

I was in a corner.

'It's not a game, Dan. It's for real,' said Joe. 'Angel's for real.'

28

A ton of revolutions later, we had a plan of sorts – one that didn't involve me getting the electric chair. Ty summarised, with Joe adding bits in.

'Call Crimestoppers from a phone box and tell them everything you know,' said Ty. He rubbed his eyes. Tiredness was still a real problem, thanks to the white van.

'Except your name,' said Joe.

'If they want evidence – to prove you're not a hoaxer, agree to call back with some,' said Ty.

'From a different phone,' said Joe.

'I haven't got any evidence,' I said.

'The code,' said Ty.

'I can't send it down the telephone wire,' I said, then quickly changed my tone. 'I could spoof an SMTP address and send them an email with the code.'

'Won't they trace it to you?' said Joe.

I shook my head.

'Play it by ear,' said Ty.

'If you've told them all you know, whatever happens afterwards isn't down to you,' said Joe.

'It's still partly his fault,' said Ty, prefect material through and through.

'Let's do it,' said Joe.

'Now?' I had an unexpectedly high voice.

'The deadline's tomorrow lunchtime,' said Joe. 'There's no time to waste.'

Oh yes there is ... Think, Dan. Think quickly.

'I can't. I need to think about what to say.'

'The truth,' said Ty, getting fed up with me.

'You wrote some code that let you control a *spy* drone, and gave it to someone called Angel. That's your script,' said Joe.

Something about the way he said it jogged an idea and sent a little current of hope through my grey matter.

'Actually there's something else I need to try first. If Angel did use my hack to steal the drone, I might be able to use it too ... maybe get it back.'

We had a short burst of raised voices. Joe saying, 'Have a go.' Ty saying, 'No, leave it to the police. You've done enough damage.' Me insisting I had to try.

'I'll have a quick look for the drone before I call the police – just in case. Then I'll use VoIP to route the call through a website from home, that's as good as a call box ... better, in fact. I'll do it when everyone's asleep. Promise.'

I hated the way I was begging, but there was a risk I'd be frogmarched to Southmead Road, and I hated that idea more.

Ty and Joe looked at each other and made a telepathic

agreement without any discernable facial movements or hand signals.

'You'd better,' said Joe.

'Let us know what happens,' said Ty.

'And let's meet tomorrow,' said Joe. 'Nine? On the corner?'

'Done,' said Ty. 'I've got to go.' He stepped off the roundabout. 'I'm bushed.'

'If you're in the clear, I'll buy you a bacon sandwich,' said Joe.

The gate clanged as we walked through it. A few streets on, we went our separate ways. I had no intention of sticking to the plan, or at least not the confessing bit. I loped home in the dark, enjoying the drop in temperature, got a packet of chocolate digestives and a Coke and set to work.

Hope is a marvellous thing.

My window into the military server via the base station was still there. Good. Once inside, I set about replicating the hack that let me control the combat drone, but ... two biscuits down, I'd already failed. The way had been locked down, barred and grilled. That meant two things. Firstly, I had no chance of finding the stolen drone. Secondly, someone somewhere — cancel that. Secondly, a cyber expert in the US Government's defence department had found the breach. And that meant they were, quite possibly, on Angel's trail. And if they were, a confession from me wouldn't help, because they already knew what I knew. All good.

The downside of my discovery was less pleasant to consider. If it wasn't Angel that was threatening the home of Big Ben, the only other person to have used that particular route in was me, so they'd be on my trail. If I hadn't been so thorough in covering my tracks, that would have been a more alarming thought. Routing through six third-party servers spread across the world made the chances of finding me miniscule. I wondered whether Angel had been as careful . . . Probably not. If he couldn't write the code, he wouldn't know how to avoid leaving footprints either. They were bound to be on to him.

It was a relief when my logical brain concluded that no action was the best plan. For all I knew, they were arresting Angel right now. By the time I saw Joe and Ty in the morning, the papers would be rejoicing in the dominance of good over evil, praising UK security for standing tall in the face of terror. (I'd make a good journalist – headlines just come to me.)

Making quips in my head in the middle of a crisis made me think of how Grandad was still cracking jokes on his deathbed. Maybe it was genetic . . . Whatever, it had to be better than the alternative, which was to collapse, wailing, 'I've ruined my life. Sob. Sob.'

29

Sleeping was out of the question. I went downstairs to get provisions for a night of ... gaming, exploring, maybe stumbling upon Angel ...

'Come in here a minute,' said Dad as I passed the door to the telly room. He was watching with Mum – rare.

'I'm just getting some —'

'Shhh!' said Dad.

Mum looked over and pressed her finger across her lips. The news was on. I felt a flutter of panic, praying it would only be the football results or a tax announcement for Dad to get all shirty about. It took a few words for me to tune in.

'. . . British Government does not negotiate with terrorists but in this instance the threat to the general public combined with the explicit nature of that threat has impelled the Secretary of State for Defence to ask for a dialogue. In this unprecedented move ...'

If I'd had dogs' ears to prick up, up they'd have gone.

'What did I miss?'

El appeared in her Hello Kitty onesie.

'He's going to bomb London,' she said. 'Like in the Blitz.'

'She's not wrong,' said Dad. 'They've decided that Dronejacker really does have a drone, and plans to use it. They want to negotiate, but in case he won't, likely targets in London are being evacuated.'

'There are helicopters and all sorts searching for the drone,' said Mum. 'Evidently they're hard to find. You wouldn't think you could lose one, would you?'

'It's a proper emergency,' said Dad. 'They've got the Eurofighters at the ready to shoot it down. Bloody terrorists.'

'How much damage can one drone do?' asked Mum.

'It's the missiles they fire, not the drones themselves,' said Dad, stating the obvious – his speciality.

'They can vaporise a car and everyone in it,' I said. 'Anyone nearby would get shrapnel damage – lose legs and arms, hearing, sight. The blast waves alone can crush your organs.'

'I'm glad *we* don't live in London,' said El. 'I don't want a bomb on my head.'

'Nor me,' I said, as casually as I could. I walked out of the door, went via the kitchen as planned, and then back upstairs. I put the Coke on my side table, took a couple of yogic breaths and read the full statement from the Secretary of State for Defence which was on the news page of the BBC, right where the terrorist had put his threat. While I waited for everyone to go to bed, I cycled through various sites. Like Dad said,

London was really jittery – no one knew whether to leg it or stay put. In a city of eight million, the chances of getting hit were tiny, but reading the sensationalist coverage, I could see why people were panicking.

There were reports of traffic jams, people abandoning cars and walking, Tube stations closed due to overcrowding, police presence outside the Houses of Parliament, Number 10, Buckingham Palace and on all the bridges. Speculation about both the likely target and the current whereabouts of the drone filled pages and pages, as did the big question: Why?

Everyone had a theory. Dronejacker was a disgruntled ex-serviceman, a fanatical Muslim, someone 'on the spectrum' like Gary McKinnon, an anti-capitalist, an anti-American, Eeyore, Kevin Bacon ... But the most plausible was that Angel was something to do with a territory that was plagued by drone strikes on civilians – Afghanistan, Pakistan, Yemen ...

By eleven-thirty the house was dark and quiet. There was no point putting off the inevitable. Angel was real. The drone was real. The threat was real. I had to do something.

But I didn't. Time ticked. I sat. How warped was Angel that he made strangers do his dirty work for him? I wanted to tie a rope round his neck, whack him with the lead piping or the spanner ... I didn't want to admit my part, own up, be brave ... but Angel made me.

The response to the government came back on the BBC's Twitter feed at midnight (using 149 characters).

The job goes ahead at noon. How does it feel, civilians, to be at the mercy of an unmanned flying weapon? By the way, Dronejacker's good. I like it.

My phone started juddering away on silent (shouldn't silent *be* silent?) but I didn't bother seeing who it was. I had nothing to say to Ruby – I'd shoved everything about her away in a little-used bit of cortex. And Joe and Ty could wait for an update. At least I'd have something to tell them when I met them at nine, thoroughly deserving my bacon sandwich.

I set up a VoIP call to Crimestoppers via a random Skype account in Dharamsala (I think the Dalai Lama lives there). A female voice answered, said she was called Rachel. I didn't give her time to say her bit, just ploughed straight in.

'I wrote some code that got control of a US drone. I gave it away to a stranger called Angel. I think he's Dronejacker.'

Confessing wasn't anything like as bad as I expected.

'And your name is?'

'I don't want to give my name.'

'That's all right. Can you tell me any more about . . . did you say Angel?'

'Yes. And no I can't. I don't know who he is.'

'Where did you meet him?'

'On lots of forums, and then on IRC. And lots of places.'

She asked me a few more questions that showed she had no idea what I was on about. My answers were all the same. No, I didn't know what he looked like. No, I had no other name for him. You get the gist.

'Can you stay on the line while I get someone else to talk to you?' she said.

Good move.

'Yes,' I said.

I waited. In front of my eyes, London's level of panic rose in pictures and words. Loads of journos, bloggers and tweeters had now drawn the same conclusion from Angel's choice of word – civilians. It fitted. Examples of drones killing innocent people were everywhere. US drones annihilated a whole wedding party in Yemen. In Pakistan, eighteen labourers were killed while they were waiting for their dinner. The military called the casualties 'collateral damage'. Anti-drone groups called them war crimes. People were angry (understandably), and one of those people was Dronejacker. If civilians *were* the target, London was right to panic.

'Hello, I'm Rick. I understand you don't want to give your name.'

'That's right,' I said.

'Can you tell me what you told my colleague, Rachel?'

I repeated what I'd said.

'That's very interesting. Thank you for calling. We'll keep an eye out for Angel, or any other callers that mention his name.'

'Is that it?' I said.

'Yes. Thank you again. Please understand that we're

very busy here today, and have other information that we need to prioritise.' There was a pause. 'We could call you back when it's quieter if you gave us a name and number . . .'

'No, thank you.'

That was the end of the conversation. He didn't believe me, had me down as a crackpot. Unless they were already hot on the tail of a well-organised gang of hackers, nothing to do with Angel.

Stop dreaming, Dan.

I looked back at Dronejacker's response to the government's attempt to negotiate. The first six words:

The job goes ahead at noon.

Stupid Dan! What did Angel always say?

good job

bad job

great job

It was him. For definite. I was involved. For definite.

Everything was pixel sharp. For the first time, I had a clear idea of what to do. I rang 101, gave my name and address, and started to tell the truth, the whole truth and nothing but the truth. (That statement is an exaggeration.)

'Can I stop you there?' said the voice. 'I need to put you through to an officer.' Who was I talking to? A school leaver on minimum wage?

I waited for, hopefully, a senior policeman . . . maybe they were putting me through to Scotland Yard . . .

The feeling that I was, at last, doing the right thing was, surprisingly, as good as when I was doing the wrong thing i.e. hijacking the spy drone. I wouldn't be treated like Gary McKinnon, because *I* was about to save the day.

'Hello, Dan,' said the voice. 'This is Police Constable Helen Perry.'

'Hi,' I said, ready to agree to them seizing my computer, phone, laptop ... Keen to be the most helpful citizen on the planet to stop London exploding in ... eight hours and eleven minutes. The squad cars were probably already on their way to me ...

'Dan, I've had a talk with my fellow officer and we think you should tell your parents about your call to us today. We could send someone round but it might be better for you to broach the subject yourself. The internet isn't the safe place it seems, Dan.'

I started to speak really quickly, explaining it all again, trying to get her to understand. But the more I spoke the more I could read her thoughts: *Poor deluded kid, probably from a troubled background.*

I found myself saying, 'I really am very clever. It wasn't that difficult once I'd found a window in Afghanistan.'

That was when I really lost her.

It's a weird feeling to not be able to convince someone you're serious. Nightmarish. Having decided to confess, being patronised like I was a little kid was frustrating as hell. I understood why people banged their heads against walls, really I did.

My word wasn't enough – I needed proof.

Leaving no footprint is an art. What I needed were dirty great muddy boots for the police to make a mould from. Not for the first time, or even the fiftieth, I wished I'd never had a conversation with Angel. Boasting about Pay As You Go online was the worst thing I'd ever done.

Hallelujah! Cancel that. It might just have been the best thing ...

30

I trawled back through my email for the only mobile number I ever got sent. All my other Pay As You Go customers had given me their numbers face to face, or via a friend, and paid cash. Angel was the only 'stranger' that I got free credit for. I had his number. His email was probably spoofed, but his number ... maybe not. I thought about ringing it, but what would I say?

'Are you the idiot with the combat drone that dragged me down with you?'

I thought about ringing PC Helen Perry but she'd got as much of a clue about me as the psychiatrist who prescribed my white pills when I was nine.

Several thoughts later, I realised that no one was going to take any notice of me unless I gave them real Angel, as opposed to virtual Angel. If his phone was still in use, and still his, I could find out where he was. First task was to identify the network and try to find him through location-based services. If not, somehow the HLR (the Home Location Register) and the VLR (Visiting Location Register) were bound to give me what I needed ... although it might take a while.

What was I waiting for?

He'll have changed his number . . . said the doubter in my head. Maybe. But I'd forgotten all about our first transaction. Maybe he had too.

Just like when I attacked the reconnaissance satellite system, first of all I tidied. It's easier to think with a calm mind (the Dalai Lama tweeted that). I put my laptop parallel with the right edge of the desk, centred my computer, shoved everything else on the floor, closed the curtains, lowered the lights (with the dimmer switch I installed myself) and randomly chose Russell Howard as background. (Music makes me sing – can't code *and* warble.) I almost got down to it in my clothes but I'd made that mistake on an all-nighter before. I grabbed my 'jama bottoms and the manky T-shirt with the washed-off reindeer on it that I like because it's soft. Ready, steady, go!

Time doesn't obey any rules when you're coding. I ate Oreos. Drank Coke. Put on 'filthy Frankie Boyle' – Mum's words – but didn't register a single gag. I needed to find what mobile operator Angel was with before I could try to find him. Servers, code, more servers. At some point I could smell my own breath – rank. I got up and fetched some water. I carried on working in silence apart from the tapping – too engrossed in the task to select more background noise.

Light filtered through the gap in the curtains. Day was close. So was I.

Angel's phone was in Norfolk! Somewhere in that lump on the right-hand side of England. The cell site gave me a five-mile circle that he was somewhere inside. But phone technology is better than that. Power levels and antenna patterns closed him down. In a city I'd have got a street, but Angel was in the middle of a lot of green. The only house, in fact.

I checked the data. Brought the location up on Google satellite. Nearest village – South Creake. The time was 7.11 (like the shop).

The doorbell went. I ran downstairs. It felt good to move even though I misjudged the last step and landed legs splayed like a newborn foal. It was the deliveryman who brings the Amazon parcels, ordered by Dad.

'Morning,' said Mum from the kitchen. I went in, dumping the package on the table.

'You're up early,' she said.

'Hungry,' I said. I had the light-headed feeling that makes everything appear not quite grounded. Eating would be good. I'd found Angel. Now I had to decide who to tell, and how to convince them.

I got a bowl and filled it with milk, about to start the Weetabix routine. Dad shuffled in wearing his fake Uggs.

'Isn't it the holidays?' he said.

I nodded.

On the radio the Today programme man that Dad likes to shout at was talking.

'London is, this morning, uncharacteristically quiet.

Many commuters have avoided the city as have —'

My spoon scraped the bottom of the bowl.

Dad said, 'Shhh!'

I moved my arm at snail speed, like an astronaut, but another look at Dad's face made me reconsider. I knew I had Angel in my sights but the rest of the world thought there was still a terror threat. I needed to shape up, get back upstairs and save the world. The report droned (ha!) on.

I abandoned the soaking-up-the-milk ritual, ate two more Weetabix in four mouthfuls, picked up my bowl, shoved it in the dishwasher and was half out of the door —

'Any plans for today?' said Mum. 'El's at holiday club so you're on your own, I'm afraid.'

The Confessional Tourette's raised its head. I mentally decapitated it.

'Revision. And I'm seeing Ty and Joe.'

'Not Ruby?' said Dad, sideways tilt of the head and a wink.

'Maybe,' I said, adopting the usual tactic of keeping everything in the garden rosy.

'See you later,' said Mum.

I escaped upstairs. The movement of the air circulated the stench from my armpits quite nicely. Old-man stink. It made sense to wait till the parents had gone out before I made THE call, so I took a shower.

The boiling hot water was better than normal. I even washed my hair.

The capital of Great Britain was quaking in fear, but a tall, thin boy in an average-sized city was about to catch the perpetrator through wile and cunning. Soon as I was dry, as long as the house was empty, I'd get on the phone to ... Scotland Yard. Why not? It was national security stuff.

I felt euphoric, like a manic-depressive in the manic bit. (Except it's bi-polar now.) (Joke: Bi-polar.com seems to be down. Oh, no sorry, it's back up again.) But somehow underneath I knew it wasn't what I should be feeling. I think the lack of sleep had got to me. It is, after all, a method of torture, affecting co-ordination, reaction time and judgement.

I had a T-shirt half over my head when the doorbell went again. I could guess who it was ... I went to let my mates in. But it was another delivery.

'John Langley,' he said.

I nodded.

'Shall I leave it round the back?'

I glanced at the huge box. What had Dad bought now?

'Yes, please.'

'Cluck, cluck,' he said, as I shut the door.

It was the chicken coop. I'd forgotten that El had negotiated no Easter eggs in exchange for being allowed four chickens.

'Scotland Yard is a metonym for the headquarters of the Metropolitan police force,' it says on their website.

'A metonym is a word, name or expression used as substitute for something else with which it is closely associated,' it says in Oxford Dictionaries.

I rang the number from the house phone, sitting on the bottom stair with my laptop on my knees. No re-routing this time. Cards on the table. A woman answered and I explained I had vital information about Dronejacker. I gave her my name and address. She put me straight through – no waiting, no music. I spoke slowly and clearly to someone from the New Cyber Crime Unit (NCCU), admitting my part in Dronejacker's plan. He didn't interrupt at all, so I found myself saying, 'Are you still there?' before I told him the best bit.

'Yes, Dan, I'm listening.'

'I know where Dronejacker is. I hacked his phone. That means I can give you GPS co-ordinates or the postcode. Both!'

There was a short silence. Not what you expect when you've just revealed the Cluedo murderer.

'OK, I'll jot down both of those now.'

Jot?

I used the International Radiotelephony Spelling Alphabet to make sure there was no mistake.

'November Romeo two one ...'

'I've got all that,' said the man from NCCU. 'Many thanks for your call, Dan.' His tone said everything. I may as well have been ringing to complain about the phone coverage in my house or the weather.

'I'm not a malicious caller. It's the truth.'

'We appreciate the call and will follow up the information you've provided. Thank you again.'

Unbelievable!

I banged my head against the newel post to see if pain helped . . . was wondering how I knew the correct name for the wooden pillar at the bottom of the stairs when the bell rang. As I twisted the latch, the door hurtled towards my face. I let out a little involuntary squeal. It was Joe, at speed. He was followed by Ty.

'You didn't find the drone, did you?' Joe asked.

I shook my head. 'The code didn't work. They must have identified the weakness in the server.'

'Will that stop Angel?' asked Ty. He was flushed. Panicky.

More head shaking. 'Not if he's already got the drone.'

'Did you call anyone?' said Joe.

I nodded. 'They didn't believe me.'

'Didn't you show them the code?' Ty was livid with me. A law-abiding boy like *him* would have known how to make them listen.

'The people who answer the phones are like . . . customer services. They don't understand. Thought I was attention-seeking. I tried Crimestoppers and the police.'

'Are you telling the truth?' asked Joe. Nice to have friends that believe in you!

'I'm not an idiot,' I said.

'Debatable,' said Joe.

'Shut up,' said Ty. 'There must be a way of showing them that you're for real.'

'There's more.' I took a deep breath in and as it whistled out I said, 'I've found Angel.'

'What?' said both voices.

I explained about the phone and showed them the street view on Google Maps. And then I explained that I'd just rung Scotland Yard.

'Brilliant,' said Ty, clearly relieved. 'Well done. Did they say what they were going to do?'

They're sending a fast black car to whisk me off to HQ where I'm going to brief the team ...

'They took the details,' I said. My voice was flat, like my mood. 'I don't think they're going to do anything.'

Ty swore – a rare thing.

'There has to be a way to get through to someone who'll realise you know what you're on about,' said Joe.

'Do what he did,' said Ty.

For once my brain was slow to interpret the short sentence that would change my life forever.

'Good one,' said Joe. 'Hack the BBC, Dan. Come on, now!'

Joe made toast and Nutella. He brought it up and the three of us sat round my computer, me coding my way to celebrity status, Ty working on the words, Joe eating.

'Add a photo of you so they can see you're normal,' said Ty.

'You'd need a photo of someone else to do that,'

said Joe, as I quickly put a hoodie over my reindeer top and dragged on jeans.

'It's not funny,' said Ty. He kept squinting, and shifting about on his chair. Even though I was the one in a mess, he was the most stressed.

What we ended up with was a headline, some explanation underneath, a picture of me, and the satellite picture of Angel's 'current whereabouts' in deepest Norfolk. The words were a bit plonky, but between us we didn't have a whole lot of experience of 'media' talk, or a lot of time, which made the hack a bit plonky too.

'Only thing is, Angel's going to see this too,' said Ty. 'He'll get away.'

'He won't get far,' I said. 'Anyway, what else can I do?'

It was 10.37 a.m. when I replicated Angel's method of communication – but I wiped the BBC's whole site. It was quicker than trying to isolate the news.

The person, known as Dronejacker, threatening to strike London at twelve noon with a missile fired from a stolen American drone calls himself Angel. He is a Black Hat. He recruited other hackers online by setting them challenges. I am one of them. I had no idea what he was planning. There are other people out there like me, I believe. We are innocent. Angel is in this house near South Creake, Fakenham, Norfolk.

I inserted the image from Google Maps and the GPS co-ordinates.

I am an elite hacker, but a White Hat. Please take me seriously. My name is Dan Langley and I live in St Albans Road, Bristol. I am 16. I tried to report him but no one took me seriously. Go and get him!

It had just gone live when Joe, who had totally got into the whole hacking scene, had an idea.

'If Angel's there now, can you see him on the spy satellite?'

'Dan's locked out, remember?' said Ty.

'Not necessarily,' I said, not bothering to explain that although I couldn't get into the server with the combat drones, last time I tried I could still get into the US Military network.

A bit of furious key-tapping later, I had not only strolled back in with my old lines of code, like I did when I was looking for the hit-and-run van, but I'd used Angel's GPS co-ordinates and found a camera covering the area.

'Is that the live feed?' asked Joe, clearly thrilled. (Makes you wonder what he'd do if he could code.)

'Yes.' I leant back in my chair. We all stared at the screen. Nothing moved. Not us. Not them.

Then the world went mad.

31

We had the satellite feed live on my computer and different browsers open on my laptop and our three phones. I won't even try to put what happened next in any order. We were everywhere. (Note the 'we'. Somehow being with Joe and Ty gave me a sense of shared responsibility.) (This was only in my head.) Calls to the house phone, mobile, on Sky News, CNN, Reuters, messages from Mum, Dad, Ruby, the subject of every new Facebook status, my name on every website, trending on Twitter with #danlangley and #dronejacker . . .

We didn't respond to anything, just watched the word spread like a virus.

'This is freaky,' said Joe.

'It's like a tsunami,' said Ty. I was thinking the same thing. My statement was the underwater earthquake, and we were seeing the rising tide – like the fact that my Pay As You Go past was already all over Twitter. Hell, even photos of me as a kid had appeared online. Wave after wave of stuff appeared.

'You should call your parents back,' said Ty.

'Mum must be delivering a baby or she'd have rung again. Dad'll be on his way home. I'll talk to him then.'

'What are you going to say?' said Joe. 'Sorry's not going to cut it.'

I laughed. It was inappropriate, like when people giggle at funerals. It's tension.

Prefect Ty started to coach me, worried about the amount of trouble I was in.

'Keep repeating the fact that you didn't know the grand plan. Make them realise —'

'Look! Something's happening.' Joe pointed at the satellite feed that was zoomed in on Angel's location. A car was driving up the road towards the isolated house. It stopped not far from the building and four figures got out and scattered. Something about the way they were moving made me suspect they were armed.

'It's a sting operation,' said Joe.

I could hear that music they play in films that makes your heart speed up, except there was no soundtrack.

Two figures approached what was presumably the front door. The other two hung back. It was hard to believe it was real. Hard to believe we were witnesses.

And then a car drew up outside *my* house. I glanced out of the window and saw the number on the roof, and blue and neon yellow all over the side. Heart-stoppingly worse, Ruby was on the other side of the road. I could already hear her friends' voices saying, 'You're better off without him.' I wanted to beat them to it, tell her they were right, but I was sorry. Tell her that I was also the sort of guy that looked after his sister and couldn't hurt a bunny rabbit.

I switched my attention back to the screen. The image wasn't angled right to see if anyone had answered the door at Angel's house.

'It's the police, Dan,' said Joe, as though I'd somehow missed the squad car outside my house.

'I can't get involved,' said Ty. 'I want to be a doctor.'

We heard the car doors shutting.

'We can go over the back,' said Joe. 'Come on.'

'OK,' said Ty. 'Good luck, mate.' He gave me a hug. Joe did the same. They left me, Dan the Hacker, to deal with the police. I looked back at the screen. The two figures at the door had disappeared – gone inside, I supposed, leaving the other two outside, one at the back, one near the road.

Did they have guns? Despite all the evidence against him, I didn't want them to actually *shoot* Angel.

The doorbell rang. I jumped, but didn't take my eyes off the screen. I was willing the Norfolk police to walk back out, escorting Angel. That's what would happen in a film. Split-second timing would mean I could answer *my* door knowing that my brave confession had made the difference. Knowing that wherever the target was in London, it was safe.

Two loud knocks on the door came next. No change on the screen.

Dad's BMW roared up the road and screeched to a halt. I heard another car do the same.

Damn! I dragged my eyes away and hurtled downstairs.

By the time I'd got to the front door, Dad was on the other side, his key making its familiar grind. I couldn't look him in the eye. I wanted to go and hide under my bed, like pets on Bonfire Night. All the certainty that I could explain away my foolishness vanished.

32

Two cars – one nee-naw, one unmarked.

Five police officers.

Two in uniform, three plain clothes.

Four men, one woman.

The time was 10.58 a.m.

'Is it true, Dan?' said Dad.

I nodded my head.

'This is a critical situation. You need to leave it to us,' said the woman. She walked in, glanced at the doors off the hall, identified the kitchen and headed that way. A hand guided me after her.

'Sit down,' she said.

I sat down, so did she. Everyone else stood, except one man who stayed in the hall. Dad hovered.

'This is how it's going to go. We're against the clock so we're going to ask some questions now. You, Dan, are going to answer them as fully as you can, as quickly as you can. You'll be taken down to the station at some point. You will get your legal representation as soon as we can get someone here but lives are at risk and that's our overriding concern, and I hope yours. Right . . .'

During her speech, beepers and phones were going off in every pocket. I could hear the man in the hall speaking but not what he was saying. I wanted to tell them that I'd seen the police at Angel's house in Norfolk so there was no need to be so serious, but surely they knew that? And anyway, I was afraid that if I opened my mouth I'd be sick, or maybe faint.

'Dan?'

I looked across at the woman and made accidental eyeball-to-eyeball contact. Shame dragged my stare down to my knees.

'I'm Inspector Janes. Dan, I need you to tell me about meeting Angel. Everything you can remember. I don't want you to judge what's useful and what isn't. You are in serious trouble, as I'm sure you realise. But you can help yourself by being honest. Let's start with what you know about the plan to steal combat drones.'

I wasn't in serious trouble. She didn't mean that. I was the good guy. Angel was trapped in a house in Norfolk with marksmen trained on all the doors and windows because of me.

'We're waiting, Dan.'

I glanced left to where Dad was leaning against the work surface. He nodded. I looked back at the policewoman. Short, dark hair, pale blue eyes, a navy suit. I focused just behind her shoulder, where I could see the jar of Marshmallow Fluff that had been left out, and started to speak. It didn't take long. I didn't tell the whole truth and nothing but the truth. Admitting the extent of the Pay As You Go scam wasn't necessary. Nor was the tiny hack when I took control of a Predator just to check whether it worked.

'You expect us to believe that you wrote some code to hack the controls of an American surveillance drone and passed it on to persons unknown without imagining they might have malicious intent?' she said.

'Yes.'

'And that you know nothing else about Angel?'

Dad's phone went off. Inspector Janes flashed him a look. He ignored the unspoken command and picked up anyway.

'Take it outside,' she said. An order.

Dad's bravado vanished, and so did he.

She checked her tablet. Asked one of the others a question. Checked again.

'OK, let's take this back to the shop,' she said.

'Dan Langley, I could arrest you on terror charges but I'm not going to . . . yet. At the moment you're voluntarily helping with our enquiries. However, you need to come with us to the station to be interviewed, and we're taking *all* your devices.'

'Can my dad come with me?' I said, stupid tears threatening to spill over my bottom lid.

'Yes, of course.'

I needed to get a grip. I needed Dan with the quips to come back and make me feel better.

Several conversations happened all at the same time.

It was agreed that Dad would follow in his car, the man in the hall confirmed that my 'brief' would be waiting at the station, and the woman in charge answered her phone, listened, and then said, 'Get onto the NCCU again. We need a digital investigator *now*.'

I was escorted upstairs with two of the men to fetch my stuff. My head was oscillating between disbelief and wanting to throw myself out of the window.

'How old are you then, Dan?' one of them asked.

'Sixteen,' I said.

'And you know how to hack a flipping drone,' he said, shaking his head.

It was a bit pointless to deny it, so I nodded.

At the top of the stairs they waited for me to see which room was Hacker's HQ.

'In here,' I said.

My curtains were still drawn. One of them went to open them. Out of habit I tapped the keyboard to wake my computer up.

'Don't touch it,' said the other one.

I dropped my arm down by my side. It immediately wanted to rise up, despite orders from my brain to stay put, because on the screen I saw a huge, dark shape pass over the cottage in Norfolk, quickly followed by two figures running to the house. I didn't have time to use words, just made a noise. The cop by my side said, 'What the ...?'

'Dr-drone,' I stuttered.

The other one moved fast, ran to the top of the

stairs and shouted for Inspector Janes. She ran up.

'What am I looking at?' she said.

Admitting guilt is hard. 'It's a satellite picture,' I said.

'Live?' she said.

I nodded. 'It's the house where Angel is. But you know that. The police are there.'

'They've just entered the property,' said the cop who'd seen what I saw.

'Describe to me what you just witnessed, Dan.'

'A large shape, that's all. Dark. Moving fast over the house.'

'I saw the same,' said the cop. 'Could be the drone … can't imagine what else it was …'

'Can you track it?' she asked me.

I shook my head. It was easier than trying to explain that sweeping satellites are no match for an object flying at speed, even knowing that the destination was London. Anyway, I had a better question for her.

'Why haven't they arrested him?'

'Angel wasn't there, Dan,' she said. 'The threat is still live.'

That was the moment. My legs went like jelly – people say that but don't really mean it. I'm not one of them. I had to lean on the back of my computer chair. I was *so* sure that Angel was in the bag. Learning that my confession was too late threw me completely.

'Where is he, then?' No one answered right away so I carried on. 'His phone was there – when I wrote that stuff on the BBC, it was there. That was ten thirty-seven.

It's . . . eleven thirteen. Look . . . it's all grass and hedges. He *must* be there.'

'Back to base,' said the inspector. 'Now.'

The two uniforms propelled me downstairs and out of the front door. I looked down in case any neighbours were staring. As I bent my head to get in the back of the unmarked car, my eyes flicked up. Ruby had gone but there were quite a few other people in the road. It was only when a camera pointed straight at me that I realised why.

We drove off, with Inspector Janes in the front, talking on the phone, and a cop in the back with me. We drew up outside Southmead Police Station. I was taken inside and led to an interview room.

'Dan Langley?' said the man in the room – dark grey suit, absolutely no smile.

'Yes.'

'I'm the duty solicitor, Graham Sommers. The only thing standing between you and a cell.'

33

The tape machine was huge and black. The inspector took a cassette – seriously, a tape – and ripped off the see-through stuff before putting it in the machine. Bang! She did the same with the other side. Bang! When she pressed the button there was a long bee-eee-eep.

'I'm Inspector Janes. Also here are ...' Everyone said their own name, me and Dad last.

'John Langley.'

'The father,' she said.

'Dan Langley,' I said.

'This interview is being taped because you are a suspect. You are not under arrest,' she said. 'You may leave at any time, although we wouldn't recommend it. You don't have to answer any questions. You are here as a volunteer.'

I was glad Dad was there to make sure they didn't turn the tape off and thump me in the guts. They all hated me. Smart-arse kid, too much time, to waste, too little idea of right and wrong.

Ten minutes into the interview, two of the officers were replaced by a cyber crime specialist called Dave and his sidekick, who'd arrived 'by chopper'.

Dave liked saying my name. And he liked it all explained, step by step. But at a pace. He smiled occasionally to encourage me, and rubbed his moustache. I kept my gaze firmly on him, because everyone else was too scary, including Dad.

'. . . so, Dan, step by step, talk me through the second stage. You'd told Angel that you'd managed to breach US Military security to watch the feed from a reconnaissance satellite.'

'That's right, because I wanted to try and see what had happened to my friend.'

'And Angel found out and then challenged you to hack a US drone?'

'Yes. No, a drone. Not a US one specifically.'

'But you chose to target an American drone?'

'Because I already knew the way in.'

Dave and his sidekick swapped glances.

'No other reason,' I added.

'OK. Explain how you went about that, Dan, step by step.'

As I talked, various people, including him, tapped their notebooks and tablets. I'd got to the bit where I'd found some big streams of data moving between Washington IP addresses and Afghanistan when the door was flung open and a huge man strode in.

'Stop the tape.'

What the hell?

The tape made a clonk.

He pointed at Dad. 'Mr Langley?'

'Yes,' said Dad.

'We need you to leave the room while we cover some confidential developments.'

'No,' said Dad. 'I'm staying with Dan. He's a child.'

I wanted to go and stand by Dad, grab his sleeve so he couldn't leave me.

'If you don't leave this room, I'll arrest Dan under the Terrorism Act *and* I'll make sure he's refused bail.'

'He can't do that, can he?' Dad appealed to the completely silent Graham Sommers, off-duty solicitor up till then . . .

'There's a drone about to fire an American missile at an unidentified target in London. Your son admits to having provided the terrorist with the wherewithal to hijack the drone.' He spoke in a monotone. 'I don't think you're in a position to argue. If people die, your son is looking at life.'

Life . . .

Dave's sidekick took Dad's arm.

'It'd be better if you came with me, sir. This situation is time-critical, as you know, and unless you want to be held along with your son . . .'

'I will remain,' said Sommers. (Not comforting.)

I opened my mouth to plead but the big guy's eyes were drilling into me. I swallowed instead.

'I'll be right outside,' said Dad. He hesitated, then said, 'If you know anything else, you *have* to tell them.'

I was left in the room with Inspector Janes, Dave

the moustache, the giant and my brief. Four against one.

The giant took a chair, turned it round and sat with his arms leaning on the backrest. He rolled up the sleeves of his jacket like a football player. And then spoke. He wasn't anything like I was expecting, luckily.

'Dan, cards on the table. Let's forget who I am and who you are and work together. I'm willing to believe you were a total idiot and supplied the code without thinking it through. I don't want to talk about that. We've got forty minutes to make absolutely sure there's nothing you've forgotten that could help avert a disaster on the scale of seven/seven. I don't want you to be scared, I want you to talk and I want you to trust me. The tape stays off. Is that all right with you?'

I nodded.

'It's just a chat,' the giant said to Graham Sommers, who nodded.

'We need to know what the target is, Dan.'

I wanted to help the giant, but I had nothing to say. I thought about confessing to the tiny hack that let me take control of the Predator, even though I knew (capital K) that it wouldn't help, when he started talking again.

'London's in chaos . . . despite the thousands that have either left or not come into the city today, there are still millions in the capital. And the Underground ticketing system's gone down . . .' Cogs started whirring, then spinning. '. . . so everyone's pouring out of the Tube onto the streets, desperate to —'

I interrupted. 'Was it a DDoS?'

Dave nodded – big moustache rub.

The giant leant closer.

'Dan, I won't be happy if you've kept information —'

'I didn't know it was connected,' I said, in a hurry to make him see I was co-operating. 'Angel was building a botnet the day he challenged me to hack the drone. But I didn't know what site he was planning on taking down. They talked about eBay and Amazon. But it would make sense wouldn't it? If no one can buy a ticket there are more people . . .' I was about to say 'in the line of fire.'

The giant looked at Dave, who took over.

'Let's go back to that day. How did you find out Angel was building a botnet?'

'They were all talking about how many bots they had.'

'Who were?'

'Angel,' I said. 'Someone called Expendable and one like a snake, not Viper but . . .'

Come on, Dan. Think!

'Anaconda – that's it.'

'Any more?'

'Yes, but I didn't notice their names.'

'How many?'

I tried to think how many people had been involved in the chat about possible targets for DDoSs.

'Eight, maybe.'

'And where did this chat take place?'

'On IRC #angeldust. Angel told me to go there, but

the channel disappeared when he did.'

'Are you sure there was no mention of London Transport?'

'None.' I shook my head for emphasis.

'Are Expendable and Anaconda friends of yours too?'

'No. I only ever met them online with Angel.'

The giant rested his elbows on the table, which brought his face close enough to headbutt me.

'Dan you've just shown us that you know more than you thought you did. I need you to think back some more. Tell us *anything* you remember Angel saying.'

All eyes on me.

'We need to know what the target is, Dan.'

Inspector Janes scrolled down on her tablet and showed the screen to the giant.

He nodded.

'Anything, Dan?' His voice was still calm but the veins in his neck were bulging.

I bit my lip. More than anything I wanted to please them . . . him, to suddenly remember Angel typing:

Buckingham Palace would be fun to bomb

Or:

one in the Eye for London

But there was nothing.

The door opened again. A woman policeman (you know what I mean) said, 'Commander, there's an update from the Met.'

'Go ahead,' said the giant, aka Commander.

'The traffic is gridlocked on all arterial routes, there's

a marked escalation in panic because of the ticketing situation, resulting in crushing injuries at pivotal stations like Kings Cross and Victoria, and reports of looting in Oxford Circus. The army are on the move.'

Even though the situation was getting worse by the minute, I felt better with the commander in control. He seemed to understand that I wasn't to blame. Only a proper crackpot would have confessed on the BBC if he was in on it.

I wracked my brains – topics we'd touched on . . . picked a random comment.

'He once said I should damage the power supply when I didn't want to go on a school trip.'

Dave asked a few more questions, but I sensed the commander was done with me. I'd told the truth. They were going to have to find Angel without me. After all, they *were* the police.

'Isn't Angel somewhere near the cottage?' I asked, suddenly braver. 'Only that's definitely where his phone was and we saw the drone . . .'

'The drone sighting is conjecture,' said the inspector.

The commander dropped a different kind of bomb.

'Angel left the cottage as soon as your announcement went live, leaving the mobile behind. She had a —'

'What do you mean "she"?' They'd got the wrong person. Angel wasn't a —

'Bring him up to speed, Inspector.'

The commander got up and wandered about with his hands in the pockets of his trousers. His stride was so long he had to turn every two steps.

'Angel is assumed to be threatening London, or specifically its civilian population, as a protest against civilian deaths attributed to drones elsewhere in the world. She is eighteen, and of Yemeni extraction. Her family is helping with our enquiries, like yourself.' The inspector paused. 'Her target could be military, governmental or simply chosen on the basis of maximum collateral damage.'

'The collateral *is* the target,' corrected the commander. 'Her grandmother was killed by an American drone, that's the motivation.'

My head was struggling to deal with the news that the 'hacking buddy' I'd spent so much time with was *female*. There's no reason why a girl can't be a hacker but being with Angel was like being with another me – it wouldn't compute. Angel didn't talk like a girl. She talked like Joe, but geekier. Wow! The whole Dronejacker thing done by ... a witch. Credit where it's due – she had me fooled on every level.

The other stuff they told me took a while to register. When it did, the roller coaster I was on took a major dive.

Real people in London, England, were going to be hit by a missile.

Murdered.

I'd been in denial, still thinking it was some kind of hoax. A Because-I-Can. Like the reciting Pi example? That's how it was for me, so I assumed it was the same for Angel. I'd flirted with the idea that he (she) was a proper terrorist, but didn't believe it deep inside . . . till now.

Knowing she had a reason changed everything. Angel wanted the world, or London at least, to know what it was like to have the threat of a Hellfire missile hanging over you. At twelve noon she was going to pulverise random individuals, just like the Americans had. How many?

Even though I didn't know what she was planning, the fact that I'd helped meant that I was an accessory to murder. But it wasn't the law that I was scared of. No way could I carry on being me, if I had blood on my hands. Kids . . . would-be doctors . . . mums with toddlers . . . old men like Ted and Isaac . . . Slain. I would never recover. And even if I did manage, after years of counselling, to come to terms with what I'd done (assuming I wasn't jailed for life) I'd be branded a killer. My mum – a killer's mum, El – a killer's sister.

Incredible – all of it.

More incredible was the fact that a commander and an inspector were sitting wasting time with me when there was a nutter on the loose . . .

'How did she get away? You *had* her.'

'She had a head start, thanks to you, Dan.' The commander's smile was ever so slightly less sincere.

'At least I found her.'

'Don't expect any praise.' He got up and went to leave the room.

'Can I go?' I asked.

I may as well not have spoken. The commander looked at the inspector.

'Chuck him in a cell,' he said.

She looked at me and repeated, in a formal tone, the legal jargon you hear on the telly.

'Dan Langley, we are detaining you for questioning on suspicion of the commission, preparation or instigation of acts of terrorism . . .'

I was under arrest.

34

They took my watch and the laces from my trainers and a few bits of crap from my pockets. It was humiliating, being treated like I'd stabbed someone, or threatened a corner-shop owner with a bat.

'Let me help,' I said, but no one listened. 'I can help. I *know* Angel.'

The cell was a room with bare walls, a shut door with a flap to speak through, a buzzer (in case of emergencies) and a bed that was actually a wide shelf, with a thin blanket. Nothing to do but think.

I couldn't tell when noon came and went. No one came to let me know what had happened. Had Angel blown up Tower Bridge? Was I partially responsible for carnage? Bodies floating in the Thames? I could see any image I felt like conjuring up in my head, thanks to the years of shooting people on X-box. I banged on the door.

'Has she done it?' I asked through the grill. 'Has she bombed London?'

'Any questions'll have to wait till you're called for,' said the voice.

I pleaded with an empty corridor.

Dad had promised he wouldn't leave. Maybe he was on the phone to a better 'brief' than Graham Sommers, trying to negotiate my release. I wanted Mum and El to come and take me home. I tried to count seconds and then minutes, to fill the time. I banged again and eventually the same policeman sauntered along – I could hear his footsteps ... slow, a stroll. I asked to go to the loo. He reluctantly let me out and accompanied me down the corridor. The urge to run was overwhelming. I had to pee while he watched. It almost wouldn't come. I thought of Ty in his hospital gown. More than anything I wanted to be normal. A boy with a girlfriend (with red hair, who goes volunteering) and mates. A boy who should be revising for his GCSEs. When we got back to the door of my cell I didn't go in straight away. I had the idea that if I crossed the threshold that would be it. Forever. People disappear. They do. I could end up in a secret court. My family could campaign for years. Mum would be grey. Dad would have a heart attack. El would qualify as a solicitor at a ridiculously young age to fight for my freedom. But I would probably already be dead. The commander looked capable of a cold-blooded murder. At least he did when he left.

Not knowing was unbearable.

Sleep would be good, I thought. You can't think, and time passes. I sat on the edge of the bed – the plastic cover creaked. I didn't want to put my head on the mattress. Lice, bed bugs, other people's hair, dribble, vomit, poo, pee, tears. I forced myself to lie down, but I stayed rigid, trying not to touch.

Let it go, Dan.

I summoned enough self-control to do a bit of yogic breathing and let my head, and then the rest of me, collapse onto the scratchy blanket. I shut my eyes tight. It was at least twenty-eight hours since I'd slept.

35

The door swinging open woke me. I had a nanosecond of disorientation and then sat up fast, flipped my legs over the side and stood.

'Can I go?' I asked, before I remembered the other pressing question. 'Did she do it?'

The officer didn't answer either.

'I'm taking you back to the interview room.'

'Please,' I said to the back of his uniform as we walked down the corridor with no windows.

He shook his head. I didn't know what that meant, so I tapped his shoulder.

'Watch it, lad,' he said, turning round. His face wasn't angry as much as bored.

'Please, can you just tell me whether Angel fired the missile?'

'No . . . she didn't. Lucky for you.'

I smiled. Couldn't help it.

Phew!

The relief felt physical, like the blood was running freely again round my body after hours of only limping.

He left me in the same room as before. There was

a clock: 5.19 p.m. The door opened and in walked Dad. Without thinking I got up and we had a hug. Rare as horse feathers – one of Grandad's sayings.

The inspector came in afterwards and gave me the good news. Free to go. Possibility of more questioning at a later date. No charges at this point. No return of phone, computer or laptop until thoroughly autopsied. Watch, laces and pocket detritus returned.

'Are you saying Dan's in the clear?' asked Dad.

'I wouldn't go as far as using the word "clear", but I can say that our priority is to locate the individual responsible for the threat.'

'Without Dan, you wouldn't know anything about Angel,' said Dad.

Go Dad!

'Dan's courage in coming forward has been noted,' she said. 'Although the outcome may have been more positive if Angel hadn't been forewarned ...'

The inspector disappeared before I could point out how many people I'd *tried* to tell.

It was only when we made it past the reception area and Dad pushed the door to let me through that I realised how awful he looked.

'Sorry.' The apology felt a bit overdue.

'We'll talk when we get home,' he said.

Dad unlocked the doors and the mirrors swung out as usual. A timely reminder of my hacking skills. He put the radio on so we didn't have to sit in silence the whole seven minutes from the police station to home.

We turned into St Albans Road. Outside our house there was a group of dark-clothed people. I saw a camera flash – realised it was the press. Dad parked in the disabled bay for next door. (First time ever.)

El was looking out of the window, but disappeared as soon as she saw us to open the front door.

'We'll have to barge through,' said Dad, getting out to face the mob. I waited until he'd got round to my side before I got out. Ignoring the questions shouted from all directions, the too-close faces and the noise of the cameras, I pushed through with Dad right beside me, batting them away.

Safely inside, he slammed the door on them.

'I was so frightened,' said El. She wrapped her arms around my middle. I hugged her, my eyes on Mum's traumatised face.

'The neighbours'll all be worried about falling house prices,' said Dad. 'No one wants to live next to a terrorist.'

Great!

The family conference took place in the kitchen. You can probably imagine it, but even if you can't I'm not going through it. There were three broad phases:

Blaming me (mostly Dad):

How could you?

Didn't you think?

What did you think she wanted it for?

Why didn't you tell us?

Did you have to confess on the BBC?

Etc.

Blaming each other:

Mum: You should have taken him to football.

Mum: You shouldn't have bought the computer.

Dad: You were more interested in El.

Dad: You don't like a row so he got away with everything.

Etc.

El taking charge:

Did you have to go to the loo in the cell?

Did they take a photo with a number?

Did they handcuff you?

Did you see any other criminals?

Etc.

Eventually Mum said, 'You must be hungry, Dan.'

'A bit.'

'Shall I make scrambled egg?'

That's what we have when we're ill.

I wanted to tell her that I felt really bad about making her upset but didn't want Dad to say I should have thought of that before I did it.

'Yes please, Mum.

Mum looked at Dad.

'Not for me,' he said. 'I'm going to build the chicken coop.'

'But it's dark,' said Mum.

'I'll get a torch.' He went out of the back door.

Mum sent El for a bath and came and sat next to me. She put her arm round my shoulder and kissed my hair.

'Oh, Dan!'

Her tears made my head wet.

'I'm really sorry, Mum.' I wanted to join in the crying, show how sorry I was, but it was a full-on debating society inside my head.

No one got hurt, so what did it matter in the end?

But people could have been hurt.

But they weren't.

Because revealing where Angel was scuppered her plan.

Maybe it did, maybe it didn't.

What do you mean?

Was she ever going to do it?

Yes, why else steal the drone?

Unless it was a hoax – to frighten people ...

Where's the drone now?

Norfolk?

Maybe it never left Germany?

What about that shape?

'Conjecture,' they'd said.

She's eighteen! They're bound to catch her.

She's eighteen and very clever.

And dangerous.

Someone blew up her grandma, but she didn't blow anyone up.

So she's a goody now?

Just saying.

She used people.

Someone blew up her grandma.

Shut up.

I had a bath after El, and went to bed. It was strange not being able to check my messages – I wanted to know if there was anything from Ruby. That was my last thought – her standing across the road when the police arrived . . . until furious banging and bell-ringing woke me up.

In my half-asleep state I thought it was the chickens arriving to live in the coop. Cock-a-doodle-doo!

I looked at my watch – 03.45.

36

There was urgent talking downstairs. Mum's footsteps.

'They say there's been a development. They need to ask some more questions,' said Mum. She was trembling. 'Dan, they're taking you to London ... there's a helicopter waiting.'

I threw on some clothes, retched in the toilet a few times, and was bundled out of the house by two men. No proper reason given. Just time for Dad to say, 'I'm getting a lawyer – someone I know – then I'll drive up after you,' and for Mum to kiss me.

'It'll be all right, Dan. We'll *make* it all right.'

No one spoke. We walked up the road to the top, and turned left towards White Tree Roundabout, where the chopper was waiting on the Downs. It was like being kidnapped. As terrifying as being kidnapped. They strapped me in and gave me some ear defenders. We took off, lots of noise and a bit of lurching. The engine gave a shudder at some point. I looked across at the officers – they ignored me, staring at their tablets and occasionally saying short sentences that I couldn't lip-read. Too soon, we were over central London. It was still dark outside when we landed on a roof — turned out to be the Met — and I was led down to an interview room, again. A smarter one, with a less obviously bolted-down table. They left me there. I couldn't imagine what it was all about. Unless they'd caught Angel and she'd said it was my idea. My plan. Maybe she said I recruited her because I knew she was originally from Yemen. Maybe they thought I had a vendetta against America because of Edward Snowden or the WikiLeaks guy.

Help! Really, I wanted to shout. I started clawing at my head, as though if I could make an opening the craziness would be able to get out. When someone eventually came along — might have been five minutes or fifty — I wanted to hug them.

Do what you like, but don't leave me on my own.

37

The American Predator was brought down over the sea somewhere south of Clacton at eighteen minutes before midnight. It had made its way from South Creake down the east coast undetected, only spotted when it changed course to head west over water towards London. Whether it was on pre-programmed automatic pilot, or Angel, who was still 'at large', had retained control of the drone, was unclear. What was clear was that it got very close ... too close ...

By the time the story was relayed to me, the panic was over. A British Eurofighter had shot the drone out of the sky. Bang! The on-board Hellfire missiles didn't detonate and no one was hurt. I thanked an unknown god, so grateful that Angel hadn't got the chance to wield the weapon I'd handed to her so proudly. I hated myself.

Other people hated me too. Two men in suits – no tape, no lawyer, no Dad – were grilling me. No pretence at being nice. They were too angry for that. A little girl, all in the name of avenging her dead grandmother, had audaciously stolen an armed drone from a superpower, flown it across the sea, taken it on a tour of Norfolk (they found various satellite recordings of it killing time), disabled London Transport with a DDoS, got the capital on the run, let the deadline pass and *almost* managed to strike her target. (It's hard not to make it sound too impressive.) She wasn't in the room to take the flak, so it all landed on me.

The men in suits were much more thorough than the commander and his crew, going through every day of my life using my computer and laptop to prompt me, using emails, other people's Facebook status updates, even the news. It didn't help.

'I didn't know anything about Angel or the plan,' I said, again. 'I thought she was a he. I thought it was a show-off thing. Hackers do that sort of stuff.'

'Are you showing off now?'

'No!'

'The game's changed, Dan,' said the slightly fatter of the identically dressed interrogators. 'The law's not clear about cyber crime against foreign governments, but an attempted drone attack on home ground . . . that's an offence we can prosecute. You're looking at charges. You're looking at a stretch inside.'

If they were trying to frighten me, it was working. Ty's prediction that I'd be the next Gary McKinnon seemed all too real.

Someone brought us coffee and toast. Guaranteed, I'll always remember where I had my first cup of hot caffeine – something I'd always avoided because of the tobacco stink. It was disgusting, as I expected.

'Once again, Dan, go through everything you can recall about the session where you were issued the challenge ...'

They kept asking the same questions in different ways, hoping I'd trip up. On what?

'How did you find out about the stolen drone?'

I gave the same answer for the nth time.

'Did you attempt to access a drone again?'

'Only because I thought I might be able to wrestle it back.' It sounded so stupid, like I was a character from a Marvel comic.

They were on me like piranhas. Stupid Dan! I'd tripped myself up. All along I'd kept the secret about the few seconds in control of a Predator ...

We went back over each hack – the spy satellite, the surveillance drone, the combat drone. Then back over the botnet scenario. It went on and on.

'Are you sure you weren't trying to join in? Two drones are better than one.'

'Why did you keep meeting Angel on #angeldust if you knew they were planning a DDoS?'

'I was interested in what they were doing,' I said. Lame. Lame.

The goading was the most difficult to deal with.

'It's an outrage that civilians are killed by drones, isn't it, Dan? You'd think the operators would be able to tell the difference between an insurgent and a little old lady? Someone should take a stand.'

Put like that, anyone would side with Angel, but I said nothing. I'd finally got the idea that the less I said, the less they could twist.

'You were in it together from the start. You helped her build the botnet, didn't you?'

In between bouts of utter despair, when I imagined they'd never let me out to breathe the Bristol air again, the thinking part of me could see that to a policeman, anyone doing anything so ... risky ... flamboyant ... just for the sake of it was unbelievable. They dealt in another world where people had proper motives – revenge, money, sex, drugs. Certainly not keyboard supremacy. We were from different planets.

'May as well get this done,' said the fatter one, wiping the droplets of sweat from his forehead.

What did he mean?

The other one got up. I shifted backwards in my chair. Unless you count the scuffle at Amelia's party, I had zero experience of being beaten up.

He turned and went out of the door.

Calm down, Dan.

'He's getting your solicitor.'

The return of Graham Sommers wasn't anything to get excited about.

Except it wasn't Graham.

'Leave us,' said the stranger, who was bald and wide and wearing an incredibly crumpled suit. 'You've ignored procedure to date but it's by the book from now on.'

That got rid of them tout de suite. I liked him already.

'Charlie Tate,' he said, sticking out his hand and smiling. 'Good to meet you, Dan. Your dad's told me what he knows but I need to hear it in your words — everything, from the beginning.'

I started at Pay As You Go, but he meant the beginning as in Adam and Eve. I whizzed through my childhood, highlighting, as he suggested, anything that could help my case. He liked the ADHD. He liked the Robin Hood angle too — stealing from the rich phone company to help the poor Soraya who shared a computer, and her friend Mia with the wicked mother.

'Detail, Dan. That's what I need.'

Detail, he got. I got some gen on him too. He knew Dad from the terraces. Never thought you met sharp-talking solicitors down at the Ashton Gate stadium!

Going back into an interview session with Charlie Tate by my side was like having a fairy godmother. He did all the talking, which suited me fine — I was bored with my own voice saying the same things. My new job was strictly 'no comment'.

Having listened to their questions for maybe an hour and given nothing back, Charlie announced, 'If you're serious about holding a sixteen-year-old savant on terror charges we need to see some substance behind the woolly allegations you're bandying around.'

I wasn't sure I liked the use of the word 'savant' — didn't that mean stratospherically clever at one thing and a dodo at everything else? Actually, maybe that was good ...

The fatter interrogator said, 'Mr Tate, with respect, your client has admitted culpability in a previous interview —'

'An admission that I will have thrown out based on his clear lack of understanding as to the implications of his act. Dan may be a gifted computer scientist but he is also a minor with a significant medical history.' A pause, for theatrical purposes. 'I suggest you let Dan go home, unless you'd like his predicament plastered over the front page of the *Daily Mail* on a slow news day.'

Charlie stood up and motioned for me to do the same.

'He will, of course, be happy to answer any further questions in my presence if the occasion arises.'

Nice!

38

Charlie drove me back to Bristol in a silver Mercedes – shiny on the outside, more like my room on the inside. He didn't tick me off, just chatted like we were mates. He said his wife was five months pregnant, so I shared the tips I'd picked up from Mum – like putting cushions under her belly for a comfortable sleep and drinking raspberry leaf tea when she's due. He seemed to find my knowledge of childbirth hilarious. I told him about Ruby too, as he was my new BFF.

'Don't lose hope,' he said. 'When it comes to love, people generally don't like what's good for them. They like what they like.'

I liked what I was hearing. Only the spectre of Dad, waiting for me with his disappointed face, sullied my mood.

'Your dad's going to meet us at the office,' said Charlie. 'He wanted to come, by the way, but I told him there was no point. Said I'd have you back from London in a jiffy.' He grinned – Cheshire-Cat-style. 'I'll bring him up to speed and then you can get off home and we'll see what happens next.'

'What do you think will happen next?'

Charlie turned to face me – not ideal when you're in the fast lane on the M4.

'They could harass you to prove a point, but given your willingness to help, I don't see that there's much mileage in that. Cyber crime is notoriously difficult to prosecute for all sorts of reasons.'

'Like?'

He puffed like a friendly dragon, eyes back on the road.

'The law hasn't caught up with the technology and never will, everyone's doing it, most people don't understand it, the evidence is either not there or incomprehensible, the internet is global but the law is most definitely local – that throws up jurisdiction issues and those alone could keep most cases in court indefinitely . . .' He took both hands off the wheel and rubbed them together. 'Great stuff for lawyers, though.'

Ding!

If Ruby ever spoke to me again and asked me what I wanted to be, I had a new answer. A lawyer, specialising in the deep, dark net . . . why not?

'So they might or might not harass me. Want to put any odds on that?' I asked.

'Odds are they'll leave you alone,' said Charlie. 'I'd put money on it. They wanted someone to kick, and without Angel, there was only you – a kid with a keyboard and no common sense. No offence!'

'None taken,' I said.

I remember the feeling his words gave me. The sense that it was definitely over. As the last few miles sped by, I wondered whether I might even end up being thanked for my part in capturing the terrorist known as Angel.

'Here we are.'

Charlie's office was in Queens Square. Dad was waiting in his car but got out as soon as we drew up.

'Are you all right, Dan?' he said. 'We were so worried.' Seeing me dragged off to London seemed, weirdly, to have made him more sympathetic.

Charlie put an arm round both of us and swept us into the building. In ten minutes he'd covered everything, reassuring Dad, and even putting in a good word for me.

'He's a bright kid. We all make mistakes, but unlike footballers, who at most break a few windows, hackers can bring down whole buildings. He's learnt his lesson.' Big wink. 'Can't be easy having all this on his conscience.'

I tried to look like I truly had learnt my lesson but actually my conscience didn't know what to make of it all. Whenever there was a crisis like the heating breaking down on Christmas morning or lost luggage at the airport, my grandad always used to say, 'Is anyone hurt?' That was all that mattered. I got that. But as Angel didn't get to fire the missiles, the only damage was to the drone. Whereas the US Military had mown down her grandma. The right and wrong of it wasn't black and white. I kept my thoughts to myself.

'I blame myself,' said Dad. 'We knew he was spending

too much time on the computer but thought he was just gaming.'

I let that slide, but we both knew the BMW's mirrors didn't hack themselves.

'All kids spend too much time on the computer,' said Charlie. 'Actually, you might want to stay offline for now, Dan. I'm sure you're aware of the extent of government surveillance operations . . . entirely unlawful.'

Dad dropped me home, where Gran was waiting. When she saw us park, she came out with a bristly broom to sweep the pavement and 'accidentally' bashed the legs and tripods of all the press. (Actually very funny – like the woman in *Tom and Jerry* whose head you never see.)

'You get back to work,' she said to Dad. 'I'll look after this one.'

Her bony arms gave me the biggest hug she could manage. 'Sit down and I'll make you a hot chocolate. Your mum's having a nap. No need to disturb her.'

She had a cup of tea and gave me her take on the situation, which was, in a nutshell: 'They deserve everything they get. If a slip of a boy can break in to the computer that controls the aeroplanes, the Americans aren't doing their job.'

Followed by: 'That drone won't be killing any more grandmothers like me and that can't be a bad thing. In the *Express* it said the poor woman was gardening!'

Gran had conveniently forgotten the part of Angel's plan that involved bombing London. She moved on to her favourite topic – the weather and its effect on her magnolia.

That hour, sitting in the kitchen with Gran, was the eye of the storm, not that we knew it. We all thought the nightmare was over. But that's the thing about storms – safe in the eye, you have no idea what's coming at you . . .

PART 2

PART 5

39

Everyone got hassled – school friends, neighbours, even the Sunday volunteers. The *Mail* wanted an interview, which Mum and Dad refused. For the money they were offering, I'd have done it, but Charlie said it was a bad idea. Other people blabbed about us quite happily. It was a case study into how you can piece together a whole life from what's freely available online and what strangers are willing to say, and get most of it wrong. I vowed to keep my future safe from social media, if I was ever allowed back on anything. Mum and Dad weren't exactly falling over themselves to let me use the home computer and who knew when mine would come winging back? It meant I could only read what was written about me in the paper – probably no bad thing.

No one seemed to know much about Angel, except that she went off the rails soon after her grandma was killed. The house in Norfolk was owned by people who'd never heard of her, bought as an investment but left empty to be commandeered by Angel. She actually grew up in Buckingham, born to a Yemeni father and a Welsh mother. They looked nice, photographed at a wedding with some people in a sort of traditional dress, and others in mini-skirts. The only picture of Angel was in school uniform, blurred so that her white socks were the most noticeable feature. Rumours were that she'd left the country to go to a training camp for terrorists – but that was the likes of the *Sun*, so entirely made up. The *Guardian*'s article suggesting she'd been recruited by fanatics and 'turned' from a happy, intelligent child into a monster was more believable. (First thing every morning, none of it was believable – Dan Langley, accomplice to terrorists. Pinch me.)

Joe was the first visitor brave enough to burrow under the blanket of paparazzi keeping the house warm. I wasn't dressed, even though it was two in the afternoon. Couldn't be bothered.

'What the hell?' he said, as he fought through the melee.

'I'm a celebrity,' I said. 'The plane's on its way to fly me to the jungle.'

He gave a satisfyingly loud laugh – first I'd heard in a while.

We went up to my room, leaving El and Mum (who was signed off work – no one wanted a baby delivered by the mother of a terrorist) making pancakes.

'You all right?' said Joe.

'I suppose so – apart from being a prisoner in my own house.'

'Better than in the nick . . . the police don't want to charge you, then?'

'With what?' I said, and then, because I remembered he was my friend, not a journalist or parent or cop, I filled him in.

'I didn't technically break any British laws because the hack was overseas and the law's fuzzy. And they believe me about not knowing what Angel was planning, so even though she got close, it doesn't change anything . . .' I shrugged. I was so bored with it all.

'There are a lot of people who think she's got a point,' he said.

'Who?'

'People who blog . . . charities . . .'

'I meant, who's got a point?'

'Angel, you idiot!'

'Really?' Gran thinking drones were evil and Americans were stupid and Angel's grandma shouldn't have been murdered was one thing, but other people agreeing . . .

'Really.' Joe gave me a knowing nod, worthy of the stage.

'Tell me,' I said.

'There are groups against using automated drones, say they're flying killer robots – they're using Angel as an example of what could happen. Amnesty, some other human rights lot, even the United Nations, have come out with statements about "collateral damage" and "drone wars". There are Afghanistanis —'

'Afghans,' I said.

'That's it. They're posting numbers of . . . you know,

normal people killed by the Americans and the British. The photo of Angel's dead grandma has gone viral – it's probably not her but ... And there's some motion or bill or something coming up in the House of Commons to stop unmanned drones flying wherever they like. It's all kicked off, Dan.'

'That was what Angel wanted,' I said. 'For people to give a damn about what happened to her family.'

'Shame she picked you to help her.'

'Tell me about it,' I said.

'Except if she hadn't, no one would have stopped her. You're the good guy,' said Joe. 'She's the terrorist.'

'It makes me sick thinking I was mates with someone who was really going to kill people. Even though I didn't meet her face to face, I thought I knew her ...'

'You didn't know she was a bird,' he said, flapping his arms.

I tried to look amused but it was too much effort. Most things were.

'Have you seen Ruby?' I heard myself ask, having promised I wasn't going to.

'No, but she rang Ty.'

'And?'

'She said she saw you being taken away. She was crying.' He winced. 'Said she didn't want anything to do with you. Sorry, mate.'

'Bet he didn't stick up for me.'

'You're not exactly flavour of the month round there either,' he said.

Throughout all the ups and downs, I'd never felt as low. I'd felt more scared, but not so completely out of hope. It looked like I'd got away with it, but I was a marked man. Even though I was the one that owned up. What were the chances of ever leading a normal life? I wasn't allowed back in school. They'd rung to say that I should stay at home and just come in for the exams. When Charlie called to see how I was he said, 'Lots of kids go to college for sixth form,' and, 'You could always use your mum's maiden name.' It would be witness protection next ...

'Are you allowed to play anything?' said Joe.

'Like?'

We ended up singing in the living room using El's karaoke thing. It was the only offline option, apart from tennis! Bizarrely, it was fun. Especially our duet of 'YMCA'. Mum came and watched. I could see she was pleased that I was out of bed and communicating.

'Would you like to stay for tea, Joe?' she asked.

I think we both had pleading eyes.

'Sure,' he said.

We had a pretty normal evening. Don't underrate it. Normal was exactly what I wanted. But normal wasn't going to last ...

The effect of that butterfly wing that fluttered way back when I was still keen on Soraya and Ty hadn't been flattened and I'd never heard of Angel or kissed Ruby or met Charlie Tate ... was silently gathering strength. There was nothing anyone could do. It was unstoppable. And I was its focus.

Days went by. I stayed inside. We ate food. Courageous neighbours came to call. Judgemental neighbours didn't. Dad fought his way to work. I revised, without Ty, which was less fun but at least gave me something to do. Actually, one day was different – the chickens arrived. El named hers Darcey Bussell, mine was Dronejacker, Mum's was Heather and Dad's, Chicken Tonight. Yep . . . side-splittingly funny!

The press interest dwindled. One morning I looked out and there was no one on the doorstep. I pulled on my jeans and, without washing, eating or cleaning my teeth, ran outside, because I had a sudden fear that I might have become agoraphobic. I crossed the road and walked to the junction with Coldharbour Road. Phew! Entirely not afraid to leave the house. A few net curtains twitched as I passed.

Terrorist on the loose!

Lock up your children!

I can't say life returned to how it was before, but my moment of global fame was over. I hung out with Joe, tried to call Ty but got no answer, or reply to my texts. I saw him at the climbing centre when I went to watch Joe competing but he stood well away from me and disappeared straight afterwards. I didn't bother with Ruby. I knew I'd see her when the exams started. That would have to do. Aiden came round with his geography books, and again with maths. Helping him helped me too. I'd changed my mind about As, I needed A*s. The lawyer idea had taken hold. I'd found out what grades you need and the A-levels to choose but, having nearly wrecked it, didn't dare mention the future. Mum didn't go back to work. No one uttered the word 'depression' but ...

Inspector Janes gave me my computers back, together with a lecture about how lucky I was to get off without charges and a warning to resist the temptation to 'fiddle'. As instructed, I restricted my activity to playing and browsing, knowing I was on a list somewhere of people to watch. Late at night I found myself reading everything there was about cyber crime:

If cyber crime was a disease, the government would have to announce a state of emergency ... – BBC

... *everyone's doing it* ... *torrenting a film on Saturday night, that's cyber crime* – random blogger

... *convicted computer hackers could be recruited to help fight cyber crime* – the Defence Secretary (virtually offering me a job).

Not that I'd work for government. I'd read enough about cover-ups, mass surveillance and what's done to whistleblowers to know whose side I was on.

40

Easter Monday was sun sun sunny. The chickens laid their first eggs – well Darcey and Heather did, the other two were protesting at their names. Dad and I collided at breakfast. Mum had gone to the supermarket with El.

'All right, Dan?' he said.

I was managing the absorption of my third Weetabix, gunning for a dry bowl.

'Fine,' I said.

'We're impressed, your mum and I, at how you've handled it.' He looked very earnest.

'Thanks,' I said.

'Working hard for your exams is the best thing you could be doing ... but you could still go volunteering.'

'As if!' I didn't mean to say that out loud.

'What do you mean?'

'Nothing,' was what I meant to say, but the Confessional Tourette's was back and this time it was in control.

'Ruby doesn't want to see me, and none of the old codgers will talk to me now I'm a terrorist.'

Dad stuttered a bit, as unused to me saying how it

really was as I was to saying it.

'You're not a terrorist. No one's pressing charges. It was a mistake. A stupid, irresponsible act. Your friends will see that, once the fuss is over.'

'Friends like Ty, you mean?' My tone was aggressive. I wanted to stop but the genie was out of the lamp.

'What's going on with him, then?'

'Have you seen him lately?' I asked. 'Have you noticed him popping round to see how I'm doing?'

That got Dad fired up too.

'Are you saying you've fallen out? Your best mate from —'

'If blanking you is falling out, then yes, we've fallen out. Big time.'

'If that's the case he can at least say it to your face. And mine. Come on, get in the car.'

Dad stood up. I didn't.

'I'm serious,' he said.

For once, Ty's dad wasn't in the middle of the tyres and pallets. At the front door, which we'd normally push at the same time as hollering, Dad rapped three times. It was excruciatingly embarrassing but I'd had no say in it. Dad was on a mission.

Ty's mum came to the door.

'Oh!'

'Hello,' said Dad. 'I thought we'd pay a visit as we haven't seen any of you for a couple of weeks ... not since Dan's bit of trouble, funnily enough.'

Her face went red. 'Well . . .' she couldn't seem to find the next word.

Ty's brothers arrived at the door. 'Hi, Dan,' they said together.

'All right?' I said.

'Come in,' said Ty's mum.

'Thank you,' said Dad.

Ty came halfway down the stairs at a pace and then slowed when he saw us. Ty's dad came out of the downstairs loo, wiping his hands on his trouser legs. That made seven of us.

'We came to see if there was some sort of problem . . . as we haven't seen you,' said Dad.

No one wanted to answer him. It was actually funny. A demonstration of how people are happy to slag you off behind your back but to your face . . .

'I'm sorry,' said Ty's mum, 'but this isn't the first time Dan's been in trouble and I don't want Ty getting involved *again*.'

I looked up at Ty. 'Mum, you're going to have to stop blaming Dan for that fight,' he said. 'We were nine, and the pumpkin started it.'

(I was Woody and Ty was Buzz. The pumpkin didn't stand a chance.)

'It's the only time I've ever been asked to come into school and I was ashamed. Anyway, this is different,' she said. 'Dan was arrested.'

'But not charged,' I said. 'Helping with enquiries in the end, that's all.'

Ty smiled. That gave me courage. I'd been kidding myself, pretending not to be bothered, but I really didn't want to lose my oldest friend and fellow *Toy Story* fan.

'I know it looked bad,' I said, 'but I had no idea what she was planning – that's why I wasn't charged. As soon as I realised Dronejacker was the person I'd been chatting to, I had no choice but to ... confess to the world.'

'That *was* brave,' said Ty, with a sideways look at his mum.

'You shouldn't have been messing with ... drones and the like, anyway,' she said. Nothing like stating the obvious.

'He knows that,' said Dad. 'And we all know Dan, don't we? Always been too clever for his own good.' (Borrowing Gran's words.) 'But he's not a terrorist, is he? So what's with the cold shoulder?'

'Everyone deserves a second chance, don't they?' said Ty, looking from one parent to another.

'That's what you always say,' added the twins, piling on the pressure.

Their mum wasn't gagging to welcome me back into the fold but what could she do?

'Do you want to come up?' said Ty. 'I'm revising. Only a week to go ...'

'Got time for a coffee?' said Ty's dad to mine.

After we'd all kissed and made up, we went straight to pick up Gran, who was coming to lunch.

'All that fuss about Dronejacker was a lot of hot air,'

she said, in the gap between finishing the roast beef and giving us our Easter eggs.

'It was a bit more than that,' said Dad.

'I remember *you* getting in a spot of trouble,' said Gran, nodding at him.

'Never,' said Dad, with a mouthful of Yorkie.

'Driving that boy's moped round the village without a helmet when I was at the shops.'

'I didn't know the rules,' said Dad. 'I was only about thirteen.'

'The apple doesn't fall far from the tree,' said Gran, winking at me.

'Of course it doesn't,' said El. 'Apples don't have wings.'

We were all happy. Oblivious to the fact that the eye had moved and we were bang in the path of the storm. Cue thunder and lightning.

41

'Good luck,' said Mum, giving me a big kiss.

'Good luck to you, too,' I said.

It was the day of my first GCSE, and Mum was finally going back to work. I'd arranged to meet Ty at the corner so we could walk together – Joe's exams didn't start for another day. I couldn't wait to see Ruby, if only to erase the memory of the last time I saw her – standing across the road. That was five weeks ago. Five weeks since Angel had been on the run. I thought about her every so often. Wondered how you eat and sleep when you're a fugitive, aged eighteen. But then again, Angel knew how to get people to do what she wanted.

'Where's your stuff?' said Ty. He had a rucksack.

I had a pen, a pencil with a rubber on the end, a calculator and a ruler in a see-through wallet in my back pocket. I whipped it out.

'No textbook?'

'We know it all, don't we?'

'You're something else,' he said, rolling his eyes.

'Doctors don't carry around books to look stuff up in, they rem-emb-er it,' I said.

He slapped me round the head and ran off. I chased and caught up with him at the entrance to Redland Park. A few other kids doing geography were on their way in, including Aiden, so we walked as a group.

There was a fair bit of joshing, only to be expected. But nothing too major. I sensed it had all been talked to death already. I was old news.

Ruby was standing, sideways on, outside the exam room. Like me, she had no bag, just a clear pencil case in her left hand. She turned, as though she knew I was looking, and smiled when she saw me. Maybe she was going to forgive me . . . I was, after all, innocent. Optimism flooded through my veins. I headed straight for her.

'Hi.' I locked my arms to the side of my body to stop me reaching out to touch her.

'Hi, Dan.'

'Got the four main forms of river erosion at the ready?' I asked, with what I hoped was an engaging grin.

'I'll talk to you like I do everyone else but that's it,' she said. 'Ty told me you were hacking and all that when we were together, so although I know you weren't part of the plot to cripple London, you're still a liar.'

'I've stopped now,' I said, with all the joy sucked out of me.

'For how long? Until the next idiot bets you can't . . . hack the president's email?'

'I mean it, Ruby. It was scary being dragged off to London and interrogated.'

'Don't expect me to feel sorry for you. You knew what you were doing was wrong.'

There was no answer that wasn't a lie, and she didn't want lies. The door opened and we trooped into the exam room. I was near the back on the right, she was further forward in the middle. Just like that day on the bus, I could see her twiddling her shiny hair and poking it behind her ear, only for it to fall forward again. I rewarded myself with a few moments staring at her between questions. The paper was easy. Even with my lovesick distractions I finished twenty minutes early. I took my eyes off Ruby and looked right, towards the windows. The vertical slatted blinds had been pulled across to keep out the sun. Through the gaps, I saw someone dressed in black and white walk past. I turned to look over my right shoulder hoping to spot the figure passing the next window. I heard the invigilator get up out of her chair but kept my stare where it was. The person in black and white flashed past, like a strobe effect.

'Keep your head facing the front,' whispered the invigilator. I did as she said.

There were loads of reasons why a uniformed policeman, or maybe it was a traffic warden, would be coming into school. A safety talk for the Year Sevens about strangers on the internet ... A careers talk ... A teacher's car parked on double yellow ...

Get a grip, Dan.

I did the yogic breathing – ten minutes and I'd be on my way home for an afternoon of biology revision.

42

'Over here, please, Dan.'

The head was standing waiting for me with an officer I recognised from the day I made my mad announcement on the world's most trusted news channel. Why had I bothered? All I'd had since I'd 'done the right thing' was hassle. If I'd stayed anonymous, they'd never have found me. I'd routed my passage through the internet so that they wouldn't even have known what country to look in, let alone which flipping number St Albans Road.

For once, I didn't feel panicked, but angry. What was so urgent that they couldn't have come to find me at home, unless they were in the game of maximum humiliation?

The policeman spoke but it was like the slatted blinds were in the way of my hearing.

'...US issued extradition request ...district judge ...arrest warrant ...reasonable grounds ...extraditable offence ...Westminster Magistrate's Court ...as soon as practical ...'

I was aware of Ruby, watching. Mr Richards was ushering everyone else along but Ruby didn't move.

'What does it mean?' I said to the head.

'I've called your father – he's on his way.'

'I need to take Dan to the station and he can talk to his father there,' said the officer. He moved as though he was going to take my arm. I stepped away.

'I don't think so,' said the head. 'It can't be that urgent. We'll wait in my office.'

He tried to protest but she hissed, 'Let's not make this any worse than it needs to be. While he is on school property, *I* make the decisions.'

She nodded at me and we walked in step, with him following. I chanced a look at Ruby. Could swear I saw tears welling up. She waved. Despite everything, seeing she cared gave me hope at what had to be another new low in my life to date. I waved back.

43

I'm going to shorthand a long, long day and night.

The Americans had asked for me to be bundled onto a plane, strip-searched and dressed in an orange boiler suit, before being thrown into one of their prisons the size of a British city because I'd made them look stupid. Or, in their words, I'd 'misused' my computer to 'break into' US Military networks and access government 'hardware', which I then shared access to. This was all explained to me, Dad and Charlie Tate at Trinity Road Police Station in St Phillips – a bit of Bristol I didn't know. As was the fact that I was expected in court the next morning, in Westminster – government territory.

Back outside, Dad and Charlie had a quick chat on the pavement about the arrangements for going to London. When Charlie shook Dad's hand, Dad held on to it.

'Surely you can't extradite a kid?' he said. 'He's sixteen!'

'Anyone can be extradited unless they are deemed too young to have committed the offence,' said Charlie.

Unreal. The whole thing was unreal.

At home, we had a subdued tea at which Dad declared, 'This family won't survive unless we keep things as normal as we can. El will go to school. We will go to work. Dan is not going to be extradited. On my life, Dan is not going anywhere.'

I liked it when he said that. It made me feel safe. Unfortunately the feeling didn't last. I spent the night lying in darkness with my head playing a loop of movie scenes mostly involving gangs of convicted murderers crowding round my cell and the guards egging them on while they beat me up. Daybreak couldn't come soon enough. By a quarter past five I was in the garden, where by some ironic miracle Dronejacker appeared to have laid her first egg.

Dad and I were driven to Westminster Magistrate's Court by Charlie, who arrived with three McDonald's breakfast baps on his lap and a tray with three coffees.

'Thanks, but I'm not sure we can eat, Charlie,' said Dad.

'Trust me, I'm a lawyer,' he said.

We'd eaten the lot by the time we got to the Swindon junction of the M4. Charlie clearly did know best.

As we drew up outside the concrete and glass building, I nearly lost it. In fact, I wanted to lose it. I wanted to be dragged in, kicking and screaming. I didn't want to have to find the courage to propel myself.

'You'll be fine,' said Charlie. 'This is a formality.'

Dad was on mute.

We went through security, up the stairs and straight in to the court. I had to stay behind a solid Perspex screen with an ugly minder, presumably so I couldn't attack anyone. When the magistrate came in, I stood, confirmed my name and she read the content of the extradition request, checking to make sure I understood what it meant.

I was granted bail to appear five weeks later, so I could finish my GCSEs first – considerate of them! The whole thing took about seven minutes.

On the way out, Charlie said, 'At least they didn't keep you in custody.' Thankfully, I hadn't realised that was an option. My clear and logical brain was finding it hard to keep all the balls in the air.

Through the huge glass doors of the building, I could see the press gathered outside. Charlie puffed up his chest, tried to smooth the crumples in his jacket and strode out to take advantage of his moment in the spotlight . . . and he was good. Dara O'Briain, but without the gags or the Irish.

'The US authorities are targeting young British geeks, of whom the latest to draw their attention is Dan Langley. Extradition laws were meant for terrorists, not kids exploring the internet from their bedrooms. The Americans would be better employed focusing their attentions on the vulnerabilities in their security systems than on those who expose them. The shabby law, passed in haste, which allows the US authorities to summon whomever they choose, is one-sided in the extreme. The burden of proof, which underpins British law, barely exists in the powers our government has handed to the Americans, in what was a poorly-thought-through knee-jerk reaction to increasing threats of terror. I would ask the Home Secretary to quickly and decisively reject the extradition request and leave Dan Langley to continue with his GCSE exams.'

Nice touch – reminding them that I was a mere schoolboy.

By quarter to twelve we were back in Bristol, having spent the journey discussing the Extradition Act 2003, punctuated by Charlie yelling at various people on his hands-free. One of the callers warned him that there were paparazzi outside his office so we went to Costa for what he called 'a proper debrief'.

'There's considerable precedent for keeping you out of the clutches of the Americans. Your age, your ADHD, and your lack of intent all work in your favour. This isn't about you, Dan, it's a cyber war. It's about Edward Snowden, it's about Julian Assange and Bradley Manning, as well as the likes of Gary McKinnon and Lauri Love. It's about secrets and surveillance, and it's about a loss of control and an escalation of fear amongst those unused to being disobeyed.'

'What are the stats?' I said, licking the chocolate powder off my top lip. 'What are the odds I win?'

'I can't say,' said Charlie. 'Ultimately, it depends on the Home Secretary – but good, the chances are good.'

'Only good?' I said, needily. (Not sure why I asked,

given how wide of the mark he was about the police leaving me alone.)

'There are no guarantees, Dan. People are fickle. Politicians more so.'

'What will happen at the hearing?' asked Dad.

'Discussion as to whether the offence is extraditable, checks of the documentation and, importantly, whether the extradition would be compatible with Dan's human rights.'

'Is it a human right to stay with your parents?' I asked. 'If you're a child.'

'The right to a family life is covered by the European Convention on Human Rights, and whilst that doesn't stop you being imprisoned, your right to regular contact should be a consideration.'

'And that would be impossible if we were here and Dan was in the States,' said Dad.

They carried on talking but I held on to my human right to have regular contact with my family. I'd never been quite so grateful to have them. (That is not a sarcastic comment.)

44

We had five weeks to wait for the full hearing. I used the time between exams to become an expert on extradition, and on the way found other hackers who had been threatened, but none that had actually ended up on American soil. It should have been comforting, but I decided that the ones that were exported to foreign jails were never heard of again. The most famous of the extradited were the NatWest Three, and the man who ran a shipping company that transported weapons. Proper criminals doing dodgy things to do with money, not people like me and my would-be BFF, Gary McKinnon. I downloaded and read his mum's book in one go – ten years it took for the Home Secretary to finally refuse the Americans. They wanted to bury him in their darkest cellar all because he left little notes inside their system ridiculing the security. He was looking for aliens on shiny spaceships – did anyone really think he represented a threat?

I tried to convince myself that, having learnt from his case, my request would be thrown out at the next hearing, but the chance, however slight, that it wouldn't be, was paralysing. I was grateful to be up to my neck in exams. Simultaneous equations, *qu'est-ce que j'aime faire pendant les vacances*, and moment = force x distance were all good at keeping my mind from straying too often to terrible places. If I wasn't revising, I was either eating or sleeping or fruitlessly searching for forgotten legislation that would guarantee I could stay in Bristol, England. The worst time of day was the morning. I'd wake up blissfully unaware that anything was wrong, and then the shadow would creep over and stay with me, until the next sleep. That was my life.

Exam number nine was on a Friday – Maths, followed by the second Geography paper in the afternoon. Not even halfway!

'Hi,' said Joe.

'All right?' I said.

We waited for Ty in silence. As time went by it got harder to chat about nothing. Not helped by the fact that I'd got into the habit of announcing the days left until Extradition Day (as I liked to call it) whenever we met.

'Remind me about graphs with equations that have squareds in,' said Joe.

I obliged. 'They're curves because a negative and a positive both end up positive when they're squared.'

'If you don't know that, you've got no hope,' said Ty, creeping up behind in his Vans.

'I don't need hope, I need facts,' said Joe.

'Three weeks and three days left,' I said. 'There's a fact.'

Ever since my day in Westminster, Ty and Joe had acted as bodyguards, sticking close in case anyone was thinking of having a pop at me. Not that anyone did. I had the impression that being a wanted man in America wasn't particularly newsworthy on top of what most of the school already knew – Pay As You Go, hacking the BBC, colluding with Angel. If you asked them, they'd probably also have accused me of dealing ketamine, carrying a knife *and* arson.

As I walked out of maths, Aiden arrived by my side. The bonding from the field trip had persisted despite my ever more criminal reputation.

'Will you go through the ecosystems chapters with me?'

'All right.'

I sat in the library with him – he was ridiculously grateful, considering I'd only helped him a handful of times.

'If I get a good grade it's *all* because of you,' he said, as we got up to go to the canteen for lunch.

I turned to find Ruby standing by the returned books shelf. She smiled, but was gone before I could say anything. She hadn't actually spoken to me since she called me a liar.

But after our geography exam, she did.

'I'm sorry about the lousy Yanks,' she said. It sounded awkward, as though she'd practised what to say.

'Me too,' I said.

'It sounds like your lawyer's good.'

'Did you see him on *Points West*?' (Somehow Charlie

had got a slot on the local news, talking about my case. I was on the way to making *him* famous.)

She nodded. 'My mum said he could do with a dry clean.'

'She's not wrong.'

We walked out of the grounds and through the park, swapping comments on the exam paper. Joe and Ty saw us together and steered clear. I was so happy to have her near me but her last words were still scabbed on the soft tissue of my brain. If she was going to be nice for five minutes but then remind me of what an idiot I'd been, I decided I might as well hear it now.

'I know I lied, pretending not to still be coding, but the thing is, Ruby, it was fun. I never thought about what I was doing. It's a pathetic excuse, but it *is* the truth. Joe's brilliant at climbing up walls, I'm brilliant at hacking. And the reason it's so ... compelling is because hackers can understand and mould stuff in a way that not even the people who first made it can.'

She made a sad face. Like she wished she could change me, but knew she couldn't.

'Will you come home with me?' I said, totally rash. 'No one's in. Not till six, anyway.' And then I used what turned out to be my trump card. 'When I'm on my own I can't stop imagining them taking me straight from the court to a holding cell at the airport.' There was an unexpected tremble in my voice.

'OK. But I want hot chocolate and —'

'Anything. You can have anything.'

45

She stayed for two hours. In my room. Door shut.
Enough said. We were back on. Big time.
Only thing was, I now had too much to lose to leave
my future to chance.

46

Ruby was on her way out of the front door when she stopped and looked at me.

'Dan, I don't go volunteering on Sundays for something to do, I go because I want the world to stay beautiful and if people don't do their bit, it won't. You need to do your bit somehow, not just wait for Charlie Tate to save you. Write a blog about extradition . . . Write a blog about how easy it is for teenagers to get sucked into the evil internet . . . Do something, Dan.'

Maybe she was right . . .

Before I had a chance to reply, we heard El yell, 'Hello, Ruby.'

She was coming up the road with Mum, obviously hyped up by after-school club because she ran up to Ruby and gave her a hug.

'I'm much better at cartwheels now. Can I show you?'

'All right,' said Ruby. 'But then I've got to go.'

El dumped her book bag in the hall and dragged Ruby out into the back garden. Sixteen cartwheels later, a dizzy El stood next to me, both of us waving to my redheaded eco-warrior as she disappeared down the road.

'See you Sunday,' I shouted.

Volunteering – all reassuringly normal.

'Nice to see Ruby here,' said Mum, a hand on my shoulder.

I nodded. 'Better get working,' I said, taking the stairs three at a time.

'It's wonderful seeing you so single-minded about doing well,' she said to my back, unaware that exams had just taken a back seat.

Right. Where to start?

Charlie Tate said there were three things in my favour – my age and my ADHD, both of which could be proved by a birth certificate and the doctor's notes, and lastly my lack of intent, which was unproven. Given that we were talking about my life (not to be too dramatic), I had to find a way to turn that third point into a fact. That had to work better than me trying to blog my way to freedom.

How to prove I was doing the equivalent of a fiendish Sudoku? Solving a puzzle with no consequences.

The fact that I ratted on Angel went some way to establishing my innocence, but a clever lawyer (we've all seen them on telly) could easily suggest that it was a double bluff, especially as I'd left it until the last moment and she got away.

Think, Dan!

Who else knew that I was only messing? Joe and Ty. Friends wouldn't make good witnesses, for obvious reasons. I needed the testimony of strangers.

Ding!

I'd been so swept up by the police going on about me and Angel that I hadn't thought much about all the other mugs who'd helped her with her plan. Like the ones that gave her bots for the DDoS on London Transport. Like the fake feed she used to steal the drone in the first place. I'd forgotten my, surely correct, theory that I was one of a group of hackers duped by Angel. She'd manipulated all of us. I needed to find the others and make them confess. How the hell I was going to do the second bit I immediately set aside to deal with later, because finding them was a task I *could* knuckle down to.

I logged on to my computer on Friday at exactly 6.30 p.m. (slightly worried that whatever I was doing was on a radar somewhere, but willing to risk it – no law against information gathering).

First stop was to join every chat room, channel, thread, forum that I'd ever been on using a new name – I picked Grey Ghost. I was desperate to declare my reason for being there but resisted. I needed to get chatting and see where we went. Whatever colour hat – white/grey/black – the others were, none of them were going to be falling over themselves to come to Westminster with me.

It didn't take long to realise that my passive strategy

was going nowhere, so I went back and started threads.

how did Dronejacker manage to pull off that whole scam?

Folk were keen to talk about it. Exploits always got a lot of interest but hacking a drone, terrorising the capital and almost striking the heart of the British Empire was up there.

I kept commenting on all the discussions, slowly turning the chat round to the idea that she'd totally played the hacking community.

Come on, someone . . . confess.

Mum interrupted my witch-hunt with spaghetti carbonara.

I ate without chewing.

'I'm on nights for the next couple of days, Dan,' said Mum.

I hardly ever look at her . . . I mean, properly look. But I did then, in between sucking the strands of pasta. She was thin and her eyes had dark shadows under them. She smiled at me, but it wasn't a happy face. It was full of fear. What had I done to my family?

I needed to get back upstairs and fix it. El's bowl was still three quarters full when I got up to leave.

'You'll get indigestion if you eat like that, Dan,' said Dad, prize burper.

'The acid comes up your feeding tube and burns and you get scars and they tighten and then you can get cancer,' said El.

'Where do you read all that stuff?' said Dad.

'Patient.co.uk,' she said.

Whichever way you looked at it, we weren't your average family.

I had a quick flick down the feeds to see if there was any joy. Nope. Just loads of talk – suggestions about how she did it, claims that it was easy, general slagging off of Americans, Yemenis, Muslims and suicide bombers . . .

The world really *is* full of crazies. Godwin's law says that the longer an online discussion goes on, the more certain it is to attract a Hitler/Nazi comparison – something to look forward to . . .

Eventually all the chats either ran out of juice or diverted onto other subjects. I gave up for the night, and Snapchatted Ruby instead. She sent a pic straight back so I Skyped her.

It felt good, lying in my bed looking at her face, hearing her laugh. Almost good enough to smother the tick of the time bomb. Almost . . .

'Why the change of heart, then, Ruby?' I asked. Brave of me.

'Same heart as before,' she said.

'Seriously, how come you decided to forgive me now . . . today?'

'Who said you were forgiven?'

'I could tell from the kissing,' I said, staring into her eyes.

She tried to hold my gaze but her eyes wouldn't obey. The rosy blush appeared on her cheeks. They should invent Skype with touch sensors.

'It was Aiden,' she said, recovering her composure.

'Aiden told you to forgive me?'

'You know I don't mean that. It was you being nice to him.'

'I am nice.'

She shifted a bit, crossed her legs and tucked a stray hair away. She was wearing a woolly jumper the colour of a sheep and what looked like washed-to-death joggers, once dark now less so. I thought of Soraya with her bright pink and purple everything – Ruby made her seem like she was from Toys R Us.

'Can you come round tomorrow?' I asked.

'Not easily.'

'Why? What are you doing?'

'Revising – Spanish.'

'You can't work all the time – in fact, you told me that. I'll come over to yours for half an hour. What do you say?'

She didn't say anything for a bit.

And then, 'I don't want my mum to know.'

I nodded in her general direction. A teenage terrorist wanted in the United States of America probably wasn't most parents' idea of an eligible suitor.

She changed the subject, and soon after said she had to go.

'See you Sunday,' I said. That would have to do.

47

'What sort of muddle have you got yourself into, Fella?' said Ted.

'It's hard to explain,' I said.

'Don't give him a hard time,' said Ruby. 'He might be deported in three weeks.'

We'd agreed that it was better to be up front.

'You seemed such a nice boy,' said Dot. 'And I pride myself on being able to judge a character.'

'He is a nice boy,' said Ruby. She was holding my hand, and her whole side was pressed against mine. Glued. I wasn't complaining.

'Leave him alone,' said Isaac. 'We're all here for the same reason – that's what matters.'

Isaac's words set the tone for the day. We travelled to a bit of coastline south of Weston where we cleaned the beach – recording how much string and plastic we found – and replaced a length of fencing that had been reported by a local rambler. It was warm. The sea was huge. We walked to the end of the jutting out bit – promontory, Isaac called it – and had cake there. I wanted to stay right where I was. Surrounded on three sides by water, and the other by Ruby.

We trundled back to Bristol on the bus, sun-baked and happy, but as I left Ruby (after some frenzied kissing), the shadow loomed, blackening my mood. I thought about being on death row – every day wondering whether it's your day for the injection that paralyses you, before the one that stops your heart. I'm pleased to say, I didn't feel quite as bad as that.

48

The days till Extradition Day flew. It was the opposite of waiting for Christmas. On the days our exams coincided, I went to the café afterwards with Ruby, but she didn't come back to mine. Her mum was on her case about revising every spare minute.

'Single mums have a lot to prove,' she said.

'Single mums should be pleased their children aren't single.'

She stuck out her tongue.

'I'll come over at the weekend,' she promised. 'And then we'll have —'

I finished the sentence. 'Seven exams left.'

She corrected me, 'More time.'

I carried on revising with Ty. He was staggered that Ruby had taken me back.

'What did you do to change her mind?'

'Copied Mandela.'

'What?'

'Truth and reconciliation.'

Charlie Tate came by one evening to see how I was doing.

'Not bad,' I said.

'I've been busy,' he said, 'lobbying. There are a lot of people angry about the unreciprocated arrangement we have with the US, particularly given the so-called *special relationship*. The Home Secretary is very aware of your case, and the fact that the British police aren't pursuing you gives us leverage. We're in a good place, Dan.'

Not good enough.

He had a beer with Dad in the kitchen and I disappeared back to my room where I carried on with my nightly quest – trawling around various sites, commenting on anything that might prompt a show-off hacker to admit his/her part in Dronejacker's plot. I was losing faith in the idea but didn't have any better ones.

Despite the hundreds of threads I'd started, I still hadn't had a Hitler comment …

But Friday night, out of the blue, KP got a message from another name I recognised – Anaconda:

I have a cell now – a Blackberry please may I have some credit like I asked you before I like your name

I had a vague memory of an infant asking me that in the Pay As You Go days, but hadn't registered the name. I had a clearer memory of Anaconda on IRC #angeldust handing over 5,000 bots. And a rock solid memory of me telling the police about it. I needed to be careful. What if it was a trick?

I looked at the post again, deciding what to do. And slapped my own forehead, really I did, when I realised she wasn't called *Anaconda*. My brain had tried to read her nonsensical arrangement of letters, and the closest it could get was the snake. In fact, she was called Annacando, which, based on my knowledge of little girls, meant Anna Can Do. It wasn't a trick – it was a variation on El's friend's YouTube channel WhatBetsyDoes. I'd found what I was looking for, another of Angel's gullible online friends. (Or rather she'd found me.)

What to do ...?

49

I quickly decided that the internet was too public to carry on any sort of conversation, given my status in the eyes of the law.

I'll call you – send your number – that was me.

no credit I get $15 a month and I spent it all on apps – Annacando.

if I get you credit will you talk to me? – I typed before I registered the dollar sign, *and* before I realised that I sounded like a groomer.

1-078-669-4634 – Annacando clearly hadn't heard of Stranger Danger.

As the old hack no longer worked, I got out my debit card, ready and willing to invest my own money in safeguarding my future, and desperately hoping you could top up a US phone from the UK.

No, was the simple answer.

I re-routed myself to an American server. Better. And then, because there's a funny system in America where the person receiving the call pays and I had no idea how much it might be, I bunged $50 on her account. As soon as the screen confirmed it had gone through, I took a deep breath and ... didn't ring Anna.

I needed a script to follow. I got a pencil and made a few notes ...

call me KP – she typed.

What the hell!

I rang the number.

'Hi, this is Anna speaking,' said a super-confident voice. 'Is that KP?'

'Yes,' I said.

'Thank you so much for the credit.'

'It's fine,' I said. It was surreal talking to a tot of a Yank. I was completely fazed about what to say. Luckily she wasn't.

'Why are you called KP?'

I explained about Club Penguin. She giggled.

'You sound real funny!'

'No, you sound funny,' I said. 'I sound English.'

'Are you calling all the way from England?'

Duh!

'No, the moon.' Unhelpful of me. I decided to move it on.

'Anna, did you collect some bots for someone called Angel?'

'I sure did. I got seven thousand or so. Do you wanna know how I did it?'

'OK.'

'I put the virus in a link for a video called "My brother poked my eye out". It was me with a patch on, holding an eye from the joke shop.'

'Cool,' I said.

'It's had fifteen thousand, four hundred and fifty-nine hits as of today. Did you also give bots to Angel?' she asked.

I was getting the idea that this little American girl didn't have a clue about Angel.

'No, I did something else for her. Do you know why she wanted the bots?'

'It was a swap. five thousand bots for four thousand, two hundred Microsoft points,' she said, missing the point.

'Anna, I need your help, but it's a bit complicated.'

'Go ahead,' she said. 'I was fifth grade "Helper of the Week" before the vacation.'

My hope that finding Annacando was the answer to a prayer had pretty much disappeared. I considered ending the call but . . .

'Are you still there, KP?'

I explained, slowly. Starting with the fact that my real name was Dan Langley, telling her what the bots had been used for (there was a squeak at that point) and ending with the fact that America – her country – wanted me to be taken away from my family.

'You mean extradited?' she said. How clever was this eleven-year-old who hadn't wondered what the bots were for?

'Yes, I didn't say it that way because I didn't know if you'd understand.'

'I'm top in my class and I'm a Gifted Youth member of American Mensa and I'm going to MIT. My papa is a professor at Harvard and my mom is a psychotherapist.'

And you need a lesson in modesty, I thought, but I didn't say anything. All of a sudden I had nothing to say. What did I expect her to do?

'How can I help you, KP?'

'I ... I hadn't really thought it through,' I said, keen to end the stupid call with the spectacle-wearing-cheesy-grin-full-of-herself-cheerleading American (not that I could see her).

'Do they want to extradite you because they think you knew what Angel was going to do?'

'Yes,' I said.

'But you didn't know. Like I didn't know that my bots were going to stop the subway?'

'That's right.'

There was a pause, longer than the lag that you get with long-distance calls, and then Anna said, 'I get it ... you want me to tell someone that I collected the bots in exchange for points, nothing to do with London, and you hacked the drone in exchange for ... what did she give you?'

'Nothing,' I said.

'That was mean,' said Anna.

I had a vision of going to Westminster Magistrate's Court with a laptop and getting Anna on Skype and having her tell the judge that she infected people's computers with her 'My brother poked my eye out' video to get points and I did it for nothing.

I heard some shouting in the distance – her end, not mine.

'Catch you later, KP,' she said. 'Mom's calling me for dinner.'

50

Saturday arrived, grey, wet and windy. It was sixteen
days until E-Day. I had scrambled eggs for breakfast,
a rare variation on the Weetabix routine, and went
back to bed. Ty arrived, with what looked like English
Lit to revise.

'Come on, we've got work to do,' he said to the slit
allowing air to reach my duvet-covered head and body.

I didn't answer so he tugged a corner, I resisted and
there was a short wrestle.

'What's the point?' I said.

'The point is that I need good grades. You can
go hang.'

'Seriously.' I sat up, cross-legged. 'What if they agree
to send me to the States?'

He shrugged. 'You can't think like that.'

I told him about my weird chat across the ocean and
now-abandoned plan to rally together Angel's army, and
played him some of AnnaCanDo's YouTube videos. The
highlight was her doing the Cinnamon Challenge and
retching. The lowlight, her solving some mathematical
thing on an Etch A Sketch. The one with the poked-out

eye wasn't there. We didn't watch her explanation of Black Holes.

'Kooky,' he said.

'She's a cross between a pageant queen and Stephen Hawking.'

'No, more like Barbie and Brian Cox.'

'Seriously, Ty, if she's anything to go by, the whole lot of us would be extradited as soon as the authorities found out about us.'

He opened his eyes wide, which made his thin pink scar crinkle.

'You thick idiot,' he said. 'Are you sure I got the brain injury and not you?'

'What are you on about?'

'What would happen if the UK asked for your American kiddy to be extradited for her part in Dronejacker's plan?'

I caught up. 'The Americans would refuse. She's only eleven, and her dad's a Harvard professor.'

'Getting better by the minute,' he said. 'And if they refuse to let her come here, no one's going to insist you go there. You can't have one rule for them and another for us. That would make the UK look pathetic.'

We talked some more – the logic was sound. If a Brit hacking a US system deserved extradition, a Yank hacking a British system deserved the same, especially as they were both part of the same plot.

Ty's smile was wider than his face. I could feel mine wasn't far off. I wanted to run round to Charlie Tate's office and tell him to do something lawyery, but it was Saturday. I tried his mobile. It was diverted.

'Calm down,' said Ty. 'Monday'll have to do.'

Ty opened a book and we somehow knuckled down to go through the play that we were going to be quizzed on in the exam on Monday. Gradually, I let the words of the Bard drown out the doubters in my head. Gradually, I started to believe that Anna could be my saviour. That the extradition papers were a step closer to being torn up and thrown away.

The doorbell rang.

'It's Ruby,' I said.

'I'll get off,' said Ty. 'See you Monday?'

'Bright and early.'

Saturday evening with Ruby and Sunday with the volunteers were the best days I'd had since the episode of Confessional Tourette's that catapulted me into the limelight. You might not think it could get better than Forgiving Friday when Ruby finally let her heart rule her head, but it did, because this time I had Ruby *and* I had hope.

51

I rang Charlie Tate and arranged to go and meet him in a café after my Monday morning exam – 1.30 in the Boston Tea Party on Park Street. I didn't tell Mum or Dad about the development but had, briefly, let myself picture Mum's relief when she realised it was properly over.

Charlie was there first, sitting on a stool by the window with his shirtsleeves rolled up, and no tie. His trousers looked like they'd been under his pillow.

'Dan!' He stood up, smiling as usual, and shook my hand. He already had a coffee in front of him, and one for me. (My third ever.)

I launched straight into the Anaconda/Annacando story, totally confusing him.

'Slow it down, Dan. Remember I'm a mortal, not a savant.'

It wasn't much better the second time but he got the basics.

'Anna is eleven, lives nears Boston, we assume, if her father teaches at Harvard, and has admitted to you, verbally, that she helped Angel build a botnet, which may have been used to bring down the London Transport ticketing capability on the day of the threatened drone strike.'

'Yes, but not *may*, *did*.'

He took a sip of coffee. Not quite the excited reaction I'd expected. I spelt it out for him.

'The US will never agree to her extradition, and that means the UK can't agree to mine or it'll look pathetic.' It sounded more convincing when Ty said it.

'Dan, our task is to keep you from being extradited. Incriminating other parties is *not* our task.' He was talking agonisingly slowly.

'But if —'

'Hear me out. I can see your thought process, but ... where do I start?' He rubbed his stubble. 'OK. Anna is in all likelihood below the age of criminal responsibility, and certainly no country would ask to extradite a child of her age. Her verbal confession of guilt to you would be inadmissible. If by a miracle she agreed to admit her part in a court of law, her lack of malicious intent, like yours, is unsubstantiated, which could make your situation worse – perhaps you were working together? To even get to that stage would be impractical in the short, or even medium term. We're talking two separate investigations, two jurisdictions, two distinctly different criminal acts and, as I've explained before, either no evidence or none that can be easily understood. The prospect of a quick and dirty tit for tat, which is I think what you were hoping for, is zero.'

I didn't want to hear excuses. I'd given him evidence and he was giving me flannel.

I raised my voice. 'I only have two weeks. That's ten lawyer days.'

'Dan, if . . . and I don't expect this to be the case . . . but *if* the extradition order is approved, we appeal. You're not going anywhere in two weeks, or two years. We stick to the plan.'

Charlie and I shook hands, and I went home. His words might have made sense to him but they didn't to me. Gary McKinnon had deportation hanging over him for ten years. In ten years I'd be twenty-six, except I wouldn't. I'd either be dead, or locked up in a mental institution. Anna was in on it, but clearly not a terrorist. There had to be some way that she could help. Hell, maybe she knew the other bot collectors . . . I hadn't thought to ask her that. By the time I got back to our empty house I had a list of questions that I should have asked the first time. She was a Gifted Youth, between us there had to be a way.

I rang her from the house phone to save my credit.

'Hi, this is Anna Rothenberg. We're hiking and wild camping, so leave a message for me, and I'll get back to you when we get home from our vacation, assuming we don't meet any bears!'

Her jolly message, so at odds with my situation, threw me completely. I ended up pleading.

'. . . I know if you admit to the botnet you'll be in trouble, but you're younger than me so nothing bad'll happen. And like I said, if you know anyone else who was involved, maybe we could all vouch for each other. I'm really scared, Anna, scared that I'll be made to leave my family and my friends.'

And Ruby.

It was truly pathetic. I flopped onto my bed, face down, and stayed there.

Without Anna, who might be in Jellystone Park with Yogi until after the hearing for all I knew, my hopes were pinned on Charlie Tate again. That didn't seem anything like as good as it had before.

My phone shuddered a few times but I stayed where I was. The pillow got wet so I turned it over.

'Dan? Are you asleep?'

It was Mum. I moved an arm to indicate that I'd heard but kept my face buried.

She came and sat on the bed and stroked my hair.

'It's hard, harder than anything any of us have been through before, but we *will* make it. We'll fight and fight. I won't lose you, Dan.'

52

You don't want a blow by blow of the countdown to E-Day. There was stress, and revision, and in between a few nice bits – sharing a large tub of Ben & Jerry's Caramel Chew Chew with Ruby, the odd hour gaming round at Joe's (Ty wouldn't come because it wasn't in his revision timetable), watching Michael McIntyre with Dad, sleeping . . . but everything was tainted by the trip to London, looming over us like the Shard.

I tried to write a blog, like Ruby suggested, but however I described what I'd done, I sounded guilty. There's a big difference between a good cause like saving the planet and what I did.

Saturday night, Dad tried to improve the family mood by taking us to The Cambridge Arms to eat. I resisted the urge to call it my 'last meal'. Ruby came with us, after ringing her mum and lying about where she was.

'How are you?' asked the barman.

'OK,' I said.

The five of us were sitting reading the menus before we chose the same as normal, when my phone delivered a message. It was Ty.

where r u
Cambridge
be there in 5

That was when a new set of dominoes started to fall, one by one.

Ty arrived with his laptop.

'I was going to show the twins Anna doing the cinnamon-eating, but when I put her name into YouTube there was a new one. Look!'

We crowded round the screen. He pressed play, and nothing happened.

'You need Wi-Fi,' said Ruby.

'They don't let you have it,' said Dad. 'It's not a library.'

'Is it something to do with the extradition?' said Mum.

Ty's nod sent Mum up to the bar and in two seconds she had the password.

Play.

There was Anna. Blonde, wavy hair, blue eyes, pink lips, tanned face, navy T-shirt. All American, in other words.

'I declare, that everything I'm about to say is true, so help me God.' She was looking straight at camera with her palm up, like it was a proper oath. 'I deliberately infected thousands of strangers' computers for someone I met on the web in exchange for points . . .' The story went on, and then got better. 'Dan Langley, who lives in England, did something for the same stranger, and like me, he didn't know what she was planning. That stranger was called Dronejacker by the news people. We thought she was called Angel. She was only discovered because

Dan tracked her down. Her real identity has been kept secret, even though she is the *only* criminal.'

Anna took a sip of water. The short silence made me aware that the whole pub was listening.

'The US Government have asked for Dan to be extradited, but that's not fair, unless I'm extradited too. Dan and I, who have never met, are not terrorists, we are only guilty of being very good at writing code and very bad at asking the questions we should have. That is not a reason to take a boy away from his sister and Mom and Dad. My parents will see this video and be mad. Please repost before they ask me to take it down, to save Dan Langley.'

Stunned. I was absolutely stunned. And moved. There was an eruption of cheers and clapping. Mum was teary. Dad was beaming. El was holding onto Ruby. People started to edge over and wish me luck. Another round of drinks came over, free of charge.

'Would you mind playing it again?' said a woman about Mum's age who had been sitting the other side of the bar. 'I didn't hear the beginning.'

Ty propped the laptop up on the counter where you order food and put the volume on max.

Afterwards the same woman got out her phone, and said, 'Anyone in the room who agrees that Dan's extradition threat is a disgrace, get sharing, blogging, tweeting, tell people . . .'

That was the second domino, falling with a great loud thump.

53

We stayed till late, all except Ruby who tried to slip away at nine-thirty but got noticed.

'Do you have to go?' said Mum. 'Dan'll happily walk you home later.'

'Her mum doesn't know about us,' I said, to save Ruby having to.

Ruby looked ashamed.

'Once Dan's in the clear, I'm sure that will . . . sort itself out,' said Mum. She leant over and kissed Ruby's cheek.

'Mum!' said El.

Dad tried to kiss El but she backed away so she was nearly sitting on Ty. All I could hear was laughing.

As soon as we got home, I went and fetched my laptop and joined Mum and Dad in the kitchen, where El was making hot chocolate for us and coffee for them.

'Don't get your hopes up,' I said. They were in a hurry to share the link, convinced the YouTube video would already have loads of views. I let them check the home computer. I was more interested in seeing if I'd had a message from Anna. I found:

I got your voice message but dont know your cell number – go to www.youtube.com/ user/annacando

I typed: **thank you so much**

'Dan, come and see.'

I shifted round a bit.

It was two hours since we'd seen the video, and four since Anna had posted it. We could hardly expect there to be thousands of hits, and there weren't. But . . . Google 'Save Dan Langley', and it was a different picture. People – people I didn't know – were talking about me. Unlike last time, when I was the devil, this time I was David and America was the big bad Goliath and Anna was my fairy godsister. I re-activated my Twitter account and wrote:

Thanks everyone #saveDanLangley

The campaign grew in real time as we watched, with hardly any trolls piling in.

'Don't underestimate the power of a pretty face,' said Dad.

'Or people's natural sense of justice,' said Mum.

'Or how much the British love an underdog.' Dad winked at me. 'How's it feel, Dan?'

I didn't have a word for it.

'Brilliant,' said El.

By midnight, Anna's plea and/or my extradition had been mentioned on human rights' sites, shared by feminists, on Mumsnet and on /digi/. The fuss only died down as Britain went to bed. About two-thirty we logged the outside world out, but not before I tweeted to Anna.

> **@Annacando #AnnaRothenberg I can never thank you enough #saveDanLangley**

It got retweeted right away. People were on my side.

I hit the pillow and for once I didn't dream about orange onesies and food in metal trays.

54

Sunday – eight days till E-Day.

Dad went and bought all the papers – just in case. I'd made the *Observer*. A politician, one in opposition, was ranting about the totally 'lopsided' Extradition Act. The article was full of numbers that basically showed that seven Brits get packed off for every one US citizen sent here. Pretty appalling given that there are tons more people living in America than Britain. Dad read the last paragraph out loud:

'All the US Attorney General has to provide, to tear sixteen-year-old Dan Langley away from his family and everything he knows, is an outline of the alleged offence, the punishment specified by statute and an accurate description of Dan himself. If Dan Langley were a US citizen, however, he would have the right to a court hearing in his home country to examine the evidence against him before any warrant was issued. The UK's National Cyber Crime Unit has questioned Dan Langley and released him without charge, yet he is due to appear at Westminster Magistrate's Court on 23rd June for an extradition hearing. Does the Home

Secretary believe this represents justice for Dan Langley?'

We ate pain au chocolat while we swapped the latest tweets, mentions and messages. People from school Snapchatted me with 'Save Dan Langley' written on their faces, walls, a thigh (that was Soraya). El was hyper – if she couldn't be famous herself, a famous brother would do.

'Can I make a Twitter account?' she asked Mum.

'I suppose so.'

She called herself @DanLangleyssister. As soon as I sent her a tweet, all my followers followed her. It was a bad decision for my reputation, but excellent for pulling heartstrings. El sent tweet after tweet saying that the chickens would miss me, and Gran would miss me, and she'd need my help on Club Penguin and loads more – all lies.

he buys me chocolate when I'm sad #saveDanLangley

he makes Mum tea in bed when she's on nights #saveDanLangley

Ruby was off with the wildlife volunteers but she called me from some bit of countryside somewhere to see how I was, which gave me an excuse to slide off to my room, lie on the bed and remember when she was in it with me.

'Isaac's filed a petition to have your case discussed in the House of Commons,' she said.

'Say thank you for me,' I said.

'Already have. I think it's going to be OK, Dan.'

'Me too,' I said.

'Got to go – we're hacking back nettles.'

'I'm not happy about you hacking.'

She snorted at my bad joke and ended the call.

I heard El running up the stairs, but before I had time to jump up and block her way she was standing with her face in mine.

'Out,' I said. 'Being nice now doesn't make up for the snot on my sock and the Facebook —'

She shoved her hand over my mouth to shut me up, pointed at my computer with her other hand and said, 'Log in.'

There was a tweet from @4liberty

@DanLangley Fast-track extradition is justice denied #saveDanLangley

'Dad said they're important.'

I knew more about 4Liberty than Dad, because the *Guardian* gets delivered on Saturdays and I occasionally read it. Dad only scans the sport and does the puzzles – enough said.

'They campaign to protect your human rights,' I told El. We went on to their website, clicked on something called 'Extradition Eyes' and read the whole thing – the press releases, the cases, the ways in which the Extradition Act 2003 was flawed, and why it should change.

I went onto 4Liberty's Facebook page to join, and spent ages reading all the notifications and messages on my page while I was there. El must have drifted away. I clicked back, intending to copy some of Liberty's stuff to show Charlie Tate, and got a surprise. They'd updated the page to put the basics of my case up there with a Twitter button to click to join the #saveDanLangley campaign.

Awesome! Hate the word, but truly, it was awesome.

55

A couple of journalists arrived before breakfast.

'Coffee?' Mum asked them – bit of a change of heart!

El took out the drinks and sat on the low wall outside our house, posing for photographs and telling them all about her plans to be a doctor. She dragged the four of us out to have a shot done together, before I headed off to my chemistry exam.

'That wasn't bad,' said Ruby afterwards.

'Was for me,' I said. 'I messed up.' No revision over the weekend, plus the media frenzy, meant I couldn't remember half the bits I *did* know.

'I could come back to yours for a bit?' she said, as Ty and Joe appeared.

'That'd be great,' I said, 'except the press are outside.' Sad face.

'We'll all come,' said Joe. 'Ruby can pretend to be with me.'

'Dream on,' she said.

While the four of us walked through the park, more dominoes were falling – dominoes the size of bricks.

No one was outside the house. The neighbour said they'd gone for fish and chips. Ruby got the bread out and shoved it in the toaster. Ty got cheese and helped himself to a lump. I got my laptop. Joe went to the loo. We had cheese and jam (Ruby's choice) on toast, washed down with Ribena at the kitchen table. I scrolled down the tweets. More of the same. Except one from @d_89johnson.

@Annacando @DanLangley And then there were three . . . youtube.com/watch?v=pVD8ac

I clicked the link.

'This might be interesting.'

He was . . . maybe fifty, American, jacket and checked shirt, actor-type face, spoke slowly and carefully, probably reading from a script.

'I am not going to say this as formally as an affidavit, although I am willing to do so if the situation regarding the young Brit, Dan Langley, does not resolve itself. My name is David Johnson and I am a research scientist at the University of Southern California. I am recording this at home in Pasadena.'

Breath.

'Around two months ago I made a video simulating a drone crashing in a wooded area for someone I believed was working on a school project. We met on an amateur videographer forum. Angel, as she was called, thanked me and I heard nothing more from her. I gave no further thought to either the video or her, until an assistant in my laboratory told me about

Anna Rothenberg. At this point I realised I too had been party to the work of Dronejacker. I believe it was my video that was used to fool the operator and replace the live feed from the drone that threatened the lives of innocent civilians in England. I have made this statement to support Dan Langley, because my conscience will not allow me to ignore his predicament. So,' he paused and looked a bit bashful before saying, 'I join Anna Rothenberg in asking you, please, to save Dan Langley!'

We laughed and laughed. We played him again, and then for fun I played him backwards. The fact that a grown-up with a good job was involved seemed to make what had happened a whole lot more believable. Kids might muck about but not the likes of David Johnson. The media felt the same. Having a new victim of Angel's cunning prompted more coverage. We were on a roll. And we hadn't even seen the *Boston Globe* by that time.

Anna Rothenberg's dad had written a piece on the opinion page. It was two o'clock British time when the article made its way across the Atlantic.

'*Although it is the involvement of my daughter, Anna, that has compelled me to declare, today, my lack of faith in the way the Extradition Act 2003 is being used, it is a view I have long held. The act was intended to expedite extradition of terror suspects in the aftermath of 9/11, not to target clever children and teenagers operating at a level above that which the lawmakers themselves can understand.*'

Wow! Big me up, why don't you?

I won't forget that afternoon. Me and my three mates sat at the table for ages, being happy. Ty temporarily abandoned his revision schedule – that's how good it felt. Charlie rang and apologised for not being more proactive when I told him about finding Anna. Ruby, before she left, said she was going to tell her mum about us as soon as the hearing was over. My mum came home with a bunch of flowers from the staff on the ward. Dad picked up El, whose class had made a good luck card for me. Supper was chatty, the shadow hardly there.

Seven days till E-Day and it was all good.

56

A *Guardian* journalist came to talk to us Tuesday evening. She had mad, wavy hair and glasses and laughed a lot.

'I want this piece to compel the Home Secretary to throw out the request before Monday's hearing. That's my raison d'être.'

She was called Amanda and we all liked her, and what she wrote. I got a snippet on the front and a whole page inside Wednesday's paper, which Ruby and I read in the café after English. She pointed at the black and white portrait.

'You're the next Johnny Depp,' she said and then laughed on her own for a few minutes.

Amanda rang me while we were saying goodbye, both going off to revise for our last paper. I planted a kiss on Ruby's lips before picking up.

'Hi.'

'Dan, Amanda here. Have you read the comments?'

'No, I've been in an exam.'

'That's something I don't miss. Check it out online. There's a distinguished list supporting your campaign.'

She wasn't wrong. The sort of faces you see in

Mail Online were dotted among the hundred or so comments. Gary McKinnon got Sting, from The Police, whereas I had Olly Murs. It was probably our age. Almost as interesting was my first Hitler reference.

If Dan Langley didn't know what he was doing Hitler didn't either

Nice to see proof of the theory.

I was lying on my bed staring at yet another vocab list, trying to care. French definitely wasn't on my list for ASs, and I was bound to do well enough in the other exams to get into sixth form. I decided to revise till tea, and read more Dan Langley web content after that. The hearing had stopped feeling like a public hanging. Everyone was convinced the Home Secretary would deny the request before I got to court. It had become a question of when. Paddy Power were taking bets on the day and time. Charlie told me that when he brought round a copy of an article he'd written in a law magazine – 'No defence of fast-track extradition'.

'Dan! El! Tea!'

I leapt up, let the book drop and raced El down the stairs. Dad was pouring wine, Mum was dishing out bowls of chilli con carne.

'Last exam tomorrow,' said Dad, as if I didn't know.

'*Oui, c'est Français.*'

'You've done well, Dan. Managing to do your exams with all this going on.'

I did the usual shrug.

Mum sat down and we tucked in.

'We all think it's going to go well,' said Dad. 'But if not, the automatic right of appeal still exists — no thanks to the government —'

'Dad just wants you to know that we're prepared,' said Mum, 'whatever happens.'

If they were trying to rein in my confidence in the campaign, it didn't work. I wasn't interested in the automatic right of appeal, because I wasn't going to need it. The world was on my side. Liberty, Friends Extradited, loads of MPs, the *Guardian*, and those were only the well-known ones.

I slept like the dead, and had to rush to get to my French exam. *Quelle horreur!* When I came out, desperate for breakfast, Charlie Tate was waiting. He ushered me to his car and got out his iPad.

'There's a fourth one about to confess.'

'How do you know?'

'There's a TV station in the States that has a morning show called *Good Day, Oregon*. They've been trailing that she's coming in for the crack of dawn slot, which is about now.'

Charlie got the video streaming from their website.

The presenter — white teeth, big salesman's smile — introduced Esther, a bookshop owner from Portland, who was enormous, with straggly hair and boho clothes. That was pretty much the only thing he managed to say. Esther was livid. Nothing to do with me. She was livid with Amazon, for cutting prices, getting exclusives, and generally killing the world's love of reading. She accused them of 'hating' books. That was why she gave Angel the bots, because she thought the plan was to take down Amazon. She didn't mention me, because she didn't care. She wanted her moment of fame to rant. It was fine by me – she was another person that Angel had lied to, which was good enough.

'Interesting,' said Charlie when the presenter finally wrestled the limelight back and we turned Esther off. 'Anna gets away with it because she's a minor. David Johnson falls between jurisdictions – aiding the hijack of an American drone on German soil, but Esther ... she was involved in the London end of the plot. That's an offence the UK could request extradition for. Dan, I think we can safely say the pressure on the Home Secretary to do something has just increased. She won't want to demand Esther's extradition because she knows it'll never happen – the US keep hold of their own – which means ...'

He chewed the right side of his lip while he waited for me to fill in the gap.

'She refuses mine.'

I got out of the car and went in search of food.

We had an end-of-exams celebration on Friday on Joe's living-room floor with the 'borrowed' projector. Ruby was rubbish, kept shooting at her feet or at me. Joe's mum got pizzas, but Ruby had to go before they were ready.

'Can't you stay?' I asked, a bit whiny.

'How can I? Mum's taking me out.'

'You are going to tell her about us, aren't you?'

Ruby nodded. 'Monday. Promise. Or sooner if . . .'

I nodded.

I left straight after tea. I'd been wired for days but, walking home, doubt started to creep back in. I hadn't made any bets with myself about when the Home Secretary would pardon me, but knowing I would wake up on Saturday with the warrant for my extradition still live wasn't in any plan. If she was going to do something, what the hell was she waiting for?

57

Friday night I didn't sleep. My head was *Prime Minister's Question Time*. All the rational arguments for rejecting the extradition were lined up but each one was shouted down. Hacker! Terrorist! Cyber-thief! I went downstairs at four in the morning and listened to the World Service, hoping for breaking news that the Home Secretary was back from a holiday and my well-being was now top of her agenda.

As the day went on, my mood, and everyone else's, dropped like the blade in an execution. We'd gone along with all the furore, imagining that the louder the noise, the surer my future was ... but that was make-believe. The reality was that I was due at an extradition hearing, Monday morning.

I told Mum not to let Ty or Joe in, and hid upstairs. I lay down on my bed but didn't shut my eyes because the orange boiler suits were back, together with the clang of a prison door and the chanting to mark a new kid being brought in, wrists and ankles handcuffed.

I thought about Angel – of everyone, only she knew I was completely innocent. But she wasn't likely to help out – it was because of me that her plan failed and she was on the run. What a crazy mess. If I'd let her carry on, we'd both be in the clear. I'd be safe – getting on with life. But a drone-sized patch of London and everyone in it would be dead or dismembered ...

It was unbearable, knowing that by trying to do the right thing I'd basically hanged myself.

I put her out of my mind – the space was immediately occupied by a torture scene set in Guantanamo Bay. I started trying to recite Pi ...

Ruby came over about six but she sobbed and so did I and in the end I asked her to go. From my bedroom window, I watched her walk down the road. She was wearing cut-off jeans, a stripy red and navy T-shirt and flip-flops. Her head was down, her hair swinging. She didn't look back.

On Sunday, when it finally dawned on everyone that the Home Secretary wasn't going to save me, two demos were arranged – one in Bristol and one in London. It gave the parents something to do. After all, I couldn't eat and didn't want to talk, and El had gone to Gran's.

I didn't go online. Too scared that the journalists would already be discussing my likely treatment in the hands of the Americans.

58

And then it *was* Extradition Day.

Mum asked me to wear a shirt. I refused. A teenager in a shirt is suspicious in itself.

Charlie picked us up in the silver Mercedes. Mum sat in the back with me, trying not to cry. Dad put on quite a good show, but we all knew how we felt. Me, I was off my head. I hadn't slept. My eyes stung. I had a headache that needed a bigger word to describe it and felt sick. And they were just the physical problems. I couldn't trust myself to speak a whole sentence without breaking down. And my head wouldn't stop playing videos of either my parents weeping as I was taken through immigration, or El hanging on to me as I was forced into a police van with blacked-out windows.

In an attempt to lessen the unbearable tension in the car, Charlie said, 'We're expecting a good turnout at the protests.'

'Great,' I said.

'It all helps,' said Dad. No one believed him.

Charlie tried again, asking Dad about the transfer

window, but small talk, even about football, had deserted us.

When we reached the Cromwell Road with its massive billboards, Charlie slowly and carefully went through the procedure again. I nodded, but it was all mashed potato. Too soon we were outside the court. My spirits rose, fleetingly, when I saw the crowds. There were at least a hundred signs, and two huge banners, held high above the heads of . . . maybe three hundred people.

There was a roar as Charlie's door opened.

Amanda from the *Guardian* was at the front.

'I won't let this drop,' she said, as the crowd moved to let us through. 'That's a promise.'

Near the door were three faces I didn't expect to see.

'We're here for you,' said Ty.

Joe nodded. 'Everyone from school's gone to the demo in Bristol.'

Ruby flung her arms around my neck and kissed me. Her face was wet. Mine was distraught.

'Good luck, Fella.'

Charlie opened the heavy glass door.

'In we go,' he said.

As it shut, it took all the noise with it, like an off switch.

We had to empty our pockets to go through the metal detectors, like last time . . . like catching an easyJet to Spain. Better not to think about planes . . .

'We're in court five this time,' said Charlie to my parents. The four of us walked over to the stairs. I stalled at the bottom step, like a horse refusing to jump.

'I can't ...'

'Don't lose it now, Dan,' said Charlie. 'For your mum.'

Somehow the wail that was rising stayed where it was. We marched up in time, like a funeral procession.

There was a bit of a wait. We sat in a row in the corridor, no one speaking.

'Breathe,' said Charlie.

The usher came along, wearing the uniform of Hogwarts, and stopped in front of us. As he opened his mouth, I prayed that he was going to deliver a last-minute reprieve, like in death row cases in films. In that split second I saw the whole scenario – a clerk running through the streets of Westminster, desperate to deliver the joyous decision (in writing, or they'd have phoned) before they strapped me down ...

'We're ready for you,' he said, arms by his sides, head slightly bowed.

I went to stand but my knees buckled. Charlie caught me.

'A second, please,' he said.

The usher moved to just beside the door.

'No one's taking you anywhere today,' said Charlie. 'Even if the decision goes against us, you still go home. Nothing happens today, Dan.'

I nodded. Mum and Dad hugged and kissed me and

I walked through the door into the court. I glanced at the judge – it was a woman this time, not young, not smiling. The usher led me into the box with the solid Perspex screen that ran from floor to ceiling. The door automatically locked as he left me inside with the security guard – not young, not smiling.

I was aware of Mum and Dad sitting in the chairs at the back, but couldn't look. There were other people too – I don't know who they were.

I leant against the backrest and caught sight of stairs – grey concrete steps, ready to lead the convicted straight from the court down to rat-infested dungeons, solitary, cells with murderers shaking the metal bars ...

Stop it, Dan.

I shifted forwards, turned so I couldn't see the stairs to hell. Caught the guard's eye, but he didn't react. I was yet another criminal.

The hearing began. The judge's voice was like a radio, stereoed into my cubicle complete with interference. I couldn't concentrate.

At some point I went on to automatic pilot, like Angel's drone when it flew down the Norfolk coast towards London. Words were spoken to me and Dan Langley's voice answered. Charlie Tate's voice rose and fell and his body weaved from side to side. The judge asked questions. The lawyer for the other side said bad words: damage, destruction, fear, terror, threats, complicit, calculating. I heard 'human rights' said again and again, but didn't feel that I had any in my Perspex box. The clerk clarified something that someone else said. I heard 'ADHD' and remembered taking the little white pills. The arguments became background, like lift music, as other memories flooded my mind. El saying her lines in the Nativity with her thumb still in her mouth. The only goal I ever scored. Eating pizza at Joe's.

I felt cold. Thought about fainting. That would be nice. Collapsing and waking up to find a nurse looking after me. Or Ruby. That would be better.

All the sound disappeared. I forced my attention back to the court. The judge was talking to the clerk, quietly. A conflab. I leant towards the screen, hoping to catch what she was saying, lip-read ...

Bent forwards, I could only get air from the very top of my lungs. I sat back, tried to make my body do the yogic breathing, but saw the steps again, imagined myself being escorted down them while Mum beat against the Perspex with her fists ... The memory of Dad trying to talk about the automatic right to appeal flashed into my mind. Was that what they were huddled together talking about? Had the Home Secretary changed the law? What if I was going straight to a holding cell at the airport? Little breaths were all that I could manage. I felt fluttery. The glass box seemed smaller.

I looked at Charlie.

Help me.

He acknowledged me, stood up to speak.

'Not a word at this stage, Mr Tate,' said the judge.

Charlie sat back down. No idea what was going on.

My eyes sought out Mum. She was leaning against Dad but straightened up when she saw me look, and pushed her hair away from her face. I wanted her to get me out of the incubator and take me home. She held on to my stare, like she was holding the whole of me.

'Stand please, Daniel.'

I did as I was told, but my eyes stayed trained on Mum.

'Daniel, you need to listen to me,' said the judge.

I didn't react.

The security guard tapped my elbow.

I forced my head round to look back at her – the woman who was allowed to decide whether I could stay with my own family in my own country.

The judge looked straight at me as she gave her decision.

'Daniel Adam Langley, I have taken into account everything that has been said on your behalf, but —' The room gasped, '— have concluded that the request of the Government of the United States of America to have you extradited to that country must be granted.'

59

'Let's go for a walk,' said Mum. 'It'll help clear your head.'

The sleeping tablet had knocked me out. Good idea of Charlie's. He was a bit of an oddball lawyer but you couldn't fault his supplies of food, drink and drugs.

'OK,' I said.

I wasn't sure when Ruby was coming over so I texted her:

going round the downs with mum – text you when back xxxxxx

My battery was on three per cent so I left my phone charging in my room, grabbed some trainers and braced myself for the heart to heart that was coming.

We'd rushed out of the court to be met by a thousand camera flashes, spent ages with Charlie going through the appeals process and zoomed back to Bristol pretty late. All Mum and Dad said before I went to bed was, 'We'll fight and fight.'

I knew *they* would, but wasn't sure how much fight I had left in me.

We dawdled up St Albans Road to North View. The man in the café waved at us with a sad face. I did one of those robot waves back, like the queen does.

'I'm proud of you, Dan. Truly, I am. You've done everything you can to put things right. It's not your fault.'

I was welling up *again*, luckily she stopped the soppy stuff just in time.

'We've got to get on with living,' she said, an upbeat voice. 'We can't let them rob us of now.'

'"*Get busy livin', or get busy dyin'*",' I said. (*The Shawshank Redemption* – Mum's favourite film.)

'Exactly.'

She put her arm through mine, and we walked in step, despite my six-inch height advantage. It's three miles to the Sea Walls and back. The sun was shining and the sky was blue, with odd streaks of white webbing. It was too early to be hot but it might be later. As usual there were joggers, dog-walkers (and dog poo), pushchairs and cyclists. It was so utterly normal, and yet not.

'If I'd had any idea, when I was messing about . . . if I'd known it would cause all this . . . all this . . . worry . . . upsetting everyone, I'd never —'

'Dan, you don't need to say anything. We understand, really . . . we do. The hack was stupid . . . teenagers are allowed to be stupid, it says so in the instructions.' She smiled. 'Remember, the police *here* agreed you have no charges to answer. *You're* not the villain, the American government is.' She paused. 'Charlie says you're a pawn in a game of chess you never agreed to play.'

'He likes to talk the talk,' I said.

Mum grinned.

'Fancy a flapjack?'

I nodded. I'd missed at least three meals.

We were by the café on the Downs. She went inside to order and I sat down at one of the round tables outside, near two men in Lycra shorts. I moved two chairs so we wouldn't have to stare at the sun – saw them look at me. They knew who I was. Mum came back out, said, 'Hello' to three women who were tying up their dogs – Bristol's like a village – and plonked the Guardian on the table. The front page was all about me.

The dark side of the "special relationship"

There was a massive photo – it was taken as I came out of the glass doors of Westminster Magistrate's Court onto the street. Ruby had her arms round my neck. You could see the side of her face, hair tucked behind her ear as usual – one way of letting her mum know! My head was on her shoulder, and my arms were wrapped round so far I looked like an orangutan. What the photo didn't show was her whispering, 'I love you, Fella.'

'Read it, then,' said Mum. 'Let's see what Amanda has to say about it all.'

I started to read aloud.

'Yesterday's decision to allow the extradition of sixteen-year-old Dan ...'

The sound of brakes made me stop reading and turn my head. Mum did the same. Two cars beeped angrily as a silver Mercedes swung across the main road and jerked to a halt. Charlie got out, waving as he walked round to the pavement side. Goosebumps, an over-fast heart rate and a dry mouth happened all at the same time. My confidence in justice had been obliterated by the court experience, leaving me convinced that if the Home Secretary clicked her fingers I'd be straight on an Airbus. Maybe today ...

'Mum?' No other words came out ...

'Don't worry.' She put her hand on my arm. 'I think he's got Gran in the front.'

The back door opened and Ruby stepped out with a massive smile. She opened the passenger door and waited for Gran. El scrambled out of the back. The four of them walked in a line across the strip of grass, the path, more grass, and the cycle path. It took a century.

'Hello,' said Mum, 'what's all this?' Her voice was jolly, but fake.

'Do either of you *ever* think of taking a phone?' said Charlie. 'I've been to every "known whereabouts" and found everyone *but* Dan.'

'Well ... you've found him now,' said Mum, still fake. *Spit it out, someone.*

I looked at Ruby, too terrified to ask. She was still smiling. Pleased to see me, or being brave ...?

'Dan!' said Charlie. His gut, which was spilling over his waistband as usual, was level with my face. I stood up. It made me feel less like a victim. It also drew everyone's attention to us – the hacking boy from yesterday's breaking news and his dishevelled lawyer.

'What is it?' I said.

Despite the traffic, Charlie's voice was the only sound. 'I have received instructions this morning from the Office of the US Attorney General, via the Home Secretary . . .' He paused to get his breath. '. . . To the effect that the extradition request has been *withdrawn*.'

He bear-hugged me.

'It's all over, Dan.'

There were silent gasps and then whooping and clapping, lots and lots of clapping. Mum put her arms round me and Charlie. I saw Gran wipe her eyes. People came out of the café to see what was going on. Hands reached over to congratulate me.

'What happened?' said Mum.

The crowd fell silent again as Charlie did what he did best.

'A few good people shamed the mighty US Government, that's what happened. A boy called Dan, who dared to admit a wrongdoing to save his fellow countrymen, a brave American called Anna, who followed his lead, her father, who took a stand against the misuse of legislation, and two other individuals, managed between them to whip up a level of support both here *and* across the pond that the powers that be were reluctant to face in the ring. Extraditing Dan would have caused a human rights *scandal*.'

'Is that what they said?' I asked, the shock making me stupid.

'Not exactly,' said Charlie, suppressing a grin. 'They

said, "The request has been revoked because of new information".'

General laughter.

The waiter came out, and had to weave between everyone to get to our table with the tray intact.

'Is it a birthday?' he asked.

El said, 'My brother can stay with us.' Her voice went high and weird and she started to cry.

'Come here,' said Gran, reaching over to give her a cuddle.

Ruby saw her chance, grabbed *me* round the neck and gave me an entirely-inappropriate-in-front-of-family kiss.

The waiter, understandably, kept his eyes down. 'Here's your hot chocolate, cappuccino, and two flapjacks . . .'

He clocked the paper, looked up.

'You're the lovebirds.'

'Tweet,' said Ruby.

He stuck his hand out to shake mine, his face as pleased as if he'd freed me himself.

'Brilliant! Absolutely brilliant! Can I get anyone else anything? Whatever anyone wants, it's on the house.'

Available in bookshops and online: Summer 2015

WHO IS ANGEL?

Samiya learnt how to fit in early on. A mixed-race
face in an all-white school doesn't have much choice.
She had no idea just how good being different could feel,
until she spent a summer in Yemen getting to know her
grandmother. It was a revelation seeing where, and how,
her father grew up. It should have been the start of
a treasured relationship, but ended up being the start
of something else. Because a month after Samiya left
Yemen, a drone fired its Hellfire missile at
her grandmother ...

So Samiya begins her campaign – writing emails,
pestering her MP, collecting names on petitions – but to
little effect. Online, talking to sympathetic strangers, she
slowly realises there's another way. She becomes Angel,
masterminding a drone attack on London.
When it fails, Angel becomes Saffron – a new city, a
new persona, short peroxide-blonde highlights and
a loving boyfriend called Liam. Can she change or is she
still Samiya, seeking revenge?

ISBN: 978 1 84812 444 8

piccadillypress.co.uk/teen

Go online to discover:

☆ more authors you'll love

☆ competitions

☆ sneak peeks inside books

☆ fun activities and downloads